RETURN OF THE REBEL DOCTOR

BY
JOANNA NEIL

WITHDRAWN

MILLS &
BOON

All the characters in this book have no existence outside the imagination of the author, and have no relation whatsoever to anyone bearing the same name or names. They are not even distantly inspired by any individual known or unknown to the author, and all the incidents are pure invention.

All Rights Reserved including the right of reproduction in whole or in part in any form. This edition is published by arrangement with Harlequin Enterprises II BV/S.à.r.l. The text of this publication or any part thereof may not be reproduced or transmitted in any form or by any means, electronic or mechanical, including photocopying, recording, storage in an information retrieval system, or otherwise, without the written permission of the publisher.

This book is sold subject to the condition that it shall not, by way of trade or otherwise, be lent, resold, hired out or otherwise circulated without the prior consent of the publisher in any form of binding or cover other than that in which it is published and without a similar condition including this condition being imposed on the subsequent purchaser.

® and TM are trademarks owned and used by the trademark owner and/or its licensee. Trademarks marked with ® are registered with the United Kingdom Patent Office and/or the Office for Harmonisation in the Internal Market and in other countries.

First published in Great Britain 2013
by Mills & Boon, an imprint of Harlequin (UK) Limited.
Harlequin (UK) Limited, Eton House,
18-24 Paradise Road, Richmond, Surrey TW9 1SR

© Joanna Neil 2013

ISBN: 978 0 263 89893 4

Harlequin (UK) policy is to use papers that are natural, renewable and recyclable products and made from wood grown in sustainable forests. The logging and manufacturing process conform to the legal environmental regulations of the country of origin.

Printed and bound in Spain
by Blackprint CPI, Barcelona

A small gasp hovered on her lips. 'You're going for the interview?' she echoed in a shocked voice.

He nodded, watching her cautiously, his expression serious. 'That's right.'

Her jaw dropped a fraction and she felt as though all the air had been sucked out of her, leaving her floundering. 'So that's why you've been hanging about all morning. You weren't here to renew old acquaintances—you were looking around, eyeing up the facilities and checking out the way we work, getting ready for any questions that might come your way this afternoon.' She was sick with disappointment. 'We're in competition for the same job.'

She'd had no idea this was coming. How could he have kept it to himself? Heavens, he might even have managed to manoeuvre her into bed with him if they hadn't been interrupted.

'We'll soon see, won't we?' She stood up, pushing her chair back and reaching for her handbag. All at once she needed to escape, and she desperately needed time to get herself ba

Essex County Council

3013020460815 1

Dear Reader

What is it that we love about a hero who is tall, dark and dangerous…dangerous to our peace of mind, that is? Is it that frisson of excitement, the secret hope that maybe our heroine is the only woman who can win his heart?

These were the questions I had in mind when I wrote Katie and Ross's story. Ross is the archetypal rebel—a man who melts women's hearts, but who is determined not to follow through. No wonder Katie tries to resist him.

And this story *had* to be set on a beautiful Scottish island—where else could my rugged hero strive to win the heart of the one woman he truly desires?

I hope you are as entranced by their story as I was when I wrote it.

Love

Joanna

When **Joanna Neil** discovered Mills & Boon®, her lifelong addiction to reading crystallised into an exciting new career writing Mills & Boon® Medical Romance™. Her characters are probably the outcome of her varied lifestyle, which includes working as a clerk, typist, nurse and infant teacher. She enjoys dressmaking and cooking at her Leicestershire home. Her family includes a husband, son and daughter, an exuberant yellow Labrador and two slightly crazed cockatiels. She currently works with a team of tutors at her local education centre, to provide creative writing workshops for people interested in exploring their own writing ambitions.

Recent titles by Joanna Neil:

HIS BRIDE IN PARADISE
TAMED BY HER BROODING BOSS
DR RIGHT ALL ALONG
DR LANGLEY: PROTECTOR OR PLAYBOY?
A COTSWOLD CHRISTMAS BRIDE
THE TAMING OF DR ALEX DRAYCOTT
BECOMING DR BELLINI'S BRIDE

These books are also available in eBook format from www.millsandboon.co.uk

**Praise for
Joanna Neil:**

'I've never given a romance novel 5 stars before,
but I loved this one.'
—*www.goodreads.com* on
A COTSWOLD CHRISTMAS BRIDE

CHAPTER ONE

'WOULD YOU COME and take a look at this young lad for me, Katie?' There was a faint note of unease in Colin McKenzie's voice, and Katie glanced up at him, wondering what could have happened to disturb the usually relaxed, easygoing police sergeant.

'Of course.' She'd been busy checking the cupboards for medical supplies, to see if there was anything she needed to reorder, but now she stopped what she was doing and turned to face him. 'What's the problem?'

She was on call at the police station a couple of evenings a week, one early, one late, which fitted in well with her shifts as a paediatrician in the emergency unit at the local hospital. Nothing much happened around here as a rule.

Being a relatively small Scottish island community, crime wasn't a major problem in the area, and Katie's role as police surgeon was generally limited to treating minor ailments, such as the occasional graze, or assessing the condition of youngsters who had drunk too much alcohol.

'It's John McGregor's boy.' Colin pulled a face. He was a tall man, with dark hair greying around the edges, the wisdom of years as a police officer weighing on his broad shoulders. 'He's been hurt. We picked him up in a raid on the Old Bakehouse—Lizzie keeps petty cash in the office there, and a gang of teenage boys were after stealing it once it got dark. The lad was acting as a lookout.'

'Finn was the lookout?' Katie sucked in a sharp breath. She'd known Finn McGregor all his life. He was a long, lanky boy, just sixteen years old, and up to now he'd managed to steer clear of any major trouble, getting off with a caution or two for things like trespass or disturbing the peace. It seemed to Katie that most of his misdeeds stemmed from youthful exuberance. Surely he couldn't have fallen in with the local troublemakers?

'How bad is it? I mean, how did he come to be injured?' She followed Colin out of the room that had been set aside as her surgery and headed with him towards the waiting room.

'It's a dog bite—not from one of our dogs, thankfully.' The sergeant looked uncomfortable. 'It was a difficult situation. He was injured, but we had to put him in the van with a police constable while we rounded up the rest of the gang. They ran off in all directions and it took us a while to catch up with them.' He grimaced.

'Anyway, in the first instance we thought about sending the lad to A and E, but that would have meant even more delay, a journey by ambulance to the hospital, and seeing as how you were on duty here...'

She nodded. 'I'll see what I can do.'

Finn was sitting on a bench at the far side of the room. He was ashen faced, blood trickling through his fingers and down his cheek as he held a thick wad of tissue paper to his ear. His grey eyes were blank with shock and his body was trembling, so that Katie's first overwhelming instinct was to go and put her arms around him and hold him close.

This was Ross's baby brother, after all—or half-brother, in truth—and she'd watched him grow from a tiny baby. Right now he looked lost and alone, and no matter what he'd done she had a compelling urge to reach out and protect him.

Sheer professionalism made her hold her instincts in check, but she went over to him and laid an arm gently around his shoulders. 'Let's go to my surgery, Finn, and I'll see if I can clean you up a bit and sort out what's to be done.'

'Oh, Katie, it's you...' Relief swamped his voice as he looked at her. 'I didn't do anything wrong, Katie, honestly.' His voice started to shake and his eyes glistened with moisture as he replayed in his mind what had happened. 'I wouldn't... I was just... And then this dog came from out of nowhere...he sank his teeth into me and wouldn't let go.' He broke off, clamping his lips together as he fought for control of himself.

'You can tell me all about it while I take a look at you,' Katie said gently. 'One thing at a time. You've had a nasty shock and we need to get you settled.'

She led him towards her medical room and sat him down on the examination couch. 'Okay,' she murmured. 'We'll just get rid of those tissues and see what's going on here. So you don't know where the dog came from?'

'No. He was just there, staring at me.' Finn let her take the blood soaked wad from him. His hands were trembling. 'I was on top of a wall,' he said, 'looking into the yard at the back of the bakehouse, when the police started shouting at me. They came for me and I jumped down.' He gulped, his voice catching with emotion. 'The dog started growling and I just froze for a moment. Then I started to run, and he leaped at me.'

Katie winced as she saw the result of the attack. The

boy's ear had been bitten right through and there were bite marks on the side of his neck. It looked a mess. 'You're going to need stitches,' she told him, 'but first of all I need to clean it up.'

Colin McKenzie hovered in the background, but as she helped Finn to lie down on the couch he said tentatively, 'Do you need any help here, Doc? Only I could send one of the constables in, if you want. Otherwise, perhaps I should go and look into this business with the dog. And there are the other lads to be questioned, paperwork to be filled in, and so on.'

She shook her head. 'I'll be fine, Sergeant. You go and do what you have to, except someone should call Finn's father and let him know what's happened. He'll need an adult to be with him.'

'Not my dad,' the boy said quickly, and Katie guessed he was afraid of how his father might react to finding he was in trouble with the police. 'He's away on business, anyway. And Mum's not well. You can't go worrying her. She's been sick with a virus these last few weeks.'

'Yes, I heard about that.' Katie frowned. Finn's mother wasn't strong, and certainly she was no match for her stern, unyielding husband. She followed his guidance where their son was concerned, and perhaps it was no wonder that Finn had begun to wander from the straight and narrow, in much the same way his half-brother had done, all those years before, though the reasons had been different in Ross's case.

'Look,' she said on a sudden impulse, 'whatever happens, Finn, I'll take care of you. I'll help you to sort this out and be with you when the police interview you, if that's what you want.' She looked at Colin, and after a moment's hesitation he nodded briefly and went out of the room.

'Thanks, Katie.' Finn bit his lip, still looking dazed as Katie began to set up her equipment, getting ready to irrigate the wound.

'I'm going to start by cleaning the wound,' she said. 'Are you okay?'

'I think so.' He frowned. 'I don't know what's going to happen now…with the police, I mean. I phoned Ross after they put me in the van. I thought he might be able to tell me what I should do.'

'You did?' Katie shot him a quick look. 'What did he say?'

'Nothing.' His shoulders slumped. 'I didn't get the chance to talk to him because the call went to voice-mail and I had to leave a message. I suppose he's busy. He's working on the mainland so I don't get to see him much these days. I just wanted to talk to him.'

She laid a hand lightly on his arm. 'I know, Finn. He seems to be settled there now, doesn't he?' She could understand the sad look in the boy's eyes. He worshipped Ross. Even though there was an age gap of around fifteen or sixteen years between them, the bond between them was very strong. But it worried Katie that the teenager was pinning his hopes on his half-brother. From what she'd heard, Ross was working in Glasgow, and it wasn't very likely that he would be able to be of much help from that distance.

She began to carefully cleanse Finn's wound. She made a thorough and painstaking job of it, and when she had finished and was satisfied with the result, she injected the area with a local anaesthetic and waited for it to take effect.

Her mind wandered, conjuring up images of Ross. All the warnings her parents had issued when she had been a young girl came flooding back to her. 'Stay away from Ross McGregor. He's trouble, mark my words,' her father had said. 'He'll come to no good, you'll see.'

A part of her had never quite been able to see Ross in that light. True, he had been the village bad boy, always up to something or other, and none of it good, but there had been a sparkle in his eyes and a quirk to his mouth that, regardless of her father's warnings, had stoked a fire inside her and made her wish for all the things she shouldn't have.

Finn shifted restlessly on the couch, and she banished those errant thoughts from her mind as she began to prepare the suture kit.

'It'll need quite a few stitches,' she told Finn, 'but I'll do my very best work so that you should be as handsome as ever once it's had a chance to heal.' She smiled, her green eyes softening as she looked at the boy.

'Maybe, when I've finished, I could get you a cup of tea. It'll help to calm your nerves. I'll have a word with Sergeant McKenzie and see if he can put off questioning you until another time.'

Finn gave an involuntary shudder. 'I don't know how I'm going to tell my dad. He won't believe I've done nothing wrong.'

Katie didn't know how to respond to that. She wouldn't have thought Finn was capable of such an unlawful act, but the sergeant must have been very sure of his misconduct to bring him in to the station.

'Well,' a familiar male voice, deep and reassuring, cut across the brief silence, 'we'll have to cross that bridge when we come to it.' Katie gave a small start of surprise. Neither of them had heard the surgery door open, but now they both stared in disbelief as Ross McGregor came into the room.

Katie's heart lurched inside her rib cage, making her

catch her breath. He was as heart-stoppingly good look-ing as ever, over six feet tall, ruggedly masculine, his strong frame clad in dark chinos and a combat jacket that could have been left over from his army days.

'I did knock,' he said, 'but perhaps you were both too engrossed to hear.' He shrugged his backpack off his shoulders and let it drop lightly to the floor. Then, as Katie turned fully towards him, his blue eyes widened. He exhaled slowly, his glance trailing in a lingering ex-ploration of her face and the cloud of bright chestnut curls that tumbled over her shoulders.

'Wow…it's great to see you again, Katie,' he said. 'I'd no idea I'd find you here. You look terrific.' He gave her a bemused nod of recognition before turning his attention to Finn.

Finn's face lit up with joy. 'You came,' he said in as-tonishment. 'How did you manage that? I didn't think you'd get my message, and I never expected you to turn up here.'

'You sounded really down, so I knew I had to come,' Ross said evenly. 'As luck had it, I managed to get the last train from Glasgow and then I took the ferry the rest of the way.' He went over to him and inspected the gaping wound left by the dog and turned to Katie. 'It looks as though you have your work cut out here. Is it all right with you if I stay and talk to Finn while you get on with the sutures?'

'That'll be fine.' She waved a hand towards the kettle on the worktop across the room. 'You could make us a hot drink—I expect you could use one after your jour-ney, and I know Finn would appreciate one when I'm done here. He can have a couple of paracetamol tablets with it to help with the pain.'

'Will do.' He strode over to the sink and filled the

kettle. 'We'll get through this, Finn,' he said. 'But first you have to tell me what happened. How did you end up in this mess?'

Finn told him his story while Katie set to work. It had been so long since she'd seen Ross, several years, in fact, but she'd heard rumours about what he'd been up to. It seemed he hadn't really changed. He was still as big and bold as ever, and the instant he'd walked into the room he'd seemed to take in the situation and assume control. He'd always been that way. He knew what he wanted, where he was headed, and nothing ever stood in his path. Not for long, anyway.

The only person who had ever had any influence over him had been his father, but Ross had put paid to any hold he'd had over him by leaving home to join the army as soon as he had been old enough. Those years had certainly left their mark on him. Now, he appeared confident, capable, and if the tales she'd heard were correct, it seemed that nothing was beyond him.

She finished the sutures and began to clear away her equipment. 'I'll put a dressing on it,' she told Finn, adding with a smile, 'I'm afraid you're going to look a bit like an Egyptian mummy for a while, with all the bandaging to hold it in place.'

'It'll just add to your street cred,' Ross told him. He waited until Katie had finished the dressing and then handed her a cup of coffee. 'Do you still take cream and sugar?' he asked, his interested gaze drifting down over her slender figure.

'Yes, please,' she murmured, his warm glance making her suddenly conscious of her feminine curves, outlined by the dress she was wearing, a simple sheath with a bodice that swathed her breasts in gentle folds of material.

To calm herself, she suggested to Finn that he should lie back against the pillows and rest awhile. 'I'll give you an anti-tetanus injection and prescribe some antibiotics in case of infection.'

Ross placed the sugar bowl and jug of cream on the table beside her. 'So, what are you doing here, Katie? Is this your regular job these days?'

She shook her head, making the soft curls quiver and dance. 'I sort of fell into this job, really. They were pushed for someone to take over when the regular surgeon had his days off, and I just happened to be in the vicinity at the time. Nowadays I fill in for the times he can't manage.'

She smiled, taking a moment to sip the coffee, enjoying the sensuous aroma. 'The rest of the time I work at the hospital in paediatric emergency medicine. I quite like the contrast, and it helps to give me a wider perspective.'

'I imagine it does.' He looked at her hand as she curved her fingers around the coffee mug. 'No ring on your finger?' he commented. 'I'd have expected you to be married, with at least a couple of children in tow, by now. Is there something wrong with the men around here?' His eyes narrowed. 'Or is there someone hovering in the wings?'

'You're very direct, aren't you?' She put down the mug, uncertain how she was going to answer him. If she gave Ross half a chance, he'd home in on her like a guided missile and lay waste to her emotions before she even knew what was coming.

'Some people would call it being nosy,' he said with a laugh, 'but I don't mind. I'm really keen to know how you're gettng on, what you've been doing these last few years. In fact...' he hesitated a moment as though he was thinking something through '...maybe we could get together for a meal or something while I'm over here? We could take some time to get to know each other all over again.'

A rush of heat ran through her at the suggestion, and she was sure her cheekbones must be highlighted with a flood of pink. Spend time with him? Get to know him all over again? Heaven forbid. Having him here in her small office had already sent her senses spinning full throttle into overdrive. How on earth would she be able to go on with her tranquil, orderly life if he was to be around for any length of time?

'Oh, I don't know about that,' she said huskily, going over to the fridge and searching for the anti-tetanus vial. Seeing the quick look of disappointment that crossed his face, she added, 'I tend to have an awful lot on these days, what with work, and renovating Waterside Cottage in my spare time. I'm actually waiting for someone to come and give me a quote for roof repairs.' They were just feeble excuses, and she guessed he knew it.

'That's a real shame.' He frowned. 'Does the cottage belong to you now? It used to be your aunt's property, didn't it—an old farmhouse that she started to renovate? I remember you and Jessie used to go and visit her there quite regularly.'

'That's right.' She went over to the couch and prepared Finn for the injection. 'Just a scratch, now. There, that's it. It's all done.'

She cleared away her equipment once more and turned back to Ross. 'It was her ongoing project,' she said with a smile. 'She never did finish everything that needed to be done, and unfortunately she died a few months ago and left the house to my sister and me. Jessie was already in the middle of buying a property for herself, though, so I bought her half from her.'

'You always liked that house, didn't you?'

She nodded, glad that the conversation had turned away from the worry of her going out on a date with him. 'There are still a few things that need doing, though, so it's turning out to be a bit of a money pit.'

'I can imagine.' He looked as though he was about to say something more, but there was a knock on the door just then, and Colin McKenzie stepped into the room.

'How's it going in here, Katie? Is the lad all right? Is he going to be fit for questioning?'

'I've patched him up, but he's not in any state to be interviewed. He's suffered a nasty injury, lost quite a lot of blood, and he's still in shock after what happened. I think we should leave him to recover for a few days, don't you?'

'Hmm.' The sergeant gave it some thought. 'Okay, I suppose you're right. I dare say no harm will come from it.' He straightened up and came further into the room, putting on his formal police officer manner as he approached the boy. 'As soon as you're finished here, you'll be bailed to appear back at this station next week to answer questions. Do you understand?'

The small amount of colour that had been in Finn's face rapidly disappeared. He didn't answer Sergeant McKenzie, but nodded in a worried fashion.

'He'll be here, along with his solicitor,' Ross said in a curt tone. 'But do you really believe he's done anything wrong, Sergeant? He said he saw the lads and was looking to see what was going on—it's pure supposition to suggest that he was acting as a lookout.'

The sergeant braced his shoulders. 'We all have a job to do, McGregor.'

'I accept that,' Ross retorted, 'but I'd have thought by now the other boys would have told you that Finn had nothing to do with the break-in.'

'Aye, but strangely they all seem to have suddenly lost any notion of who was with them,' the sergeant answered with feeling. 'To hear them talk, they were all there looking to see what was going on.'

Ross's mouth twitched faintly. 'Well, in Finn's case, if he says he knows nothing about the break-in, I'm quite sure that he's telling you the truth. Anyway, I'll be here with him when you decide to question him.'

The sergeant's brows rose. 'You're planning on staying around, then? What about your work on the mainland? You're a doctor now, aren't you, at the hospital?'

'That's right, but I've some time off owing to me, so I'm planning on taking it now.' He inclined his head in the direction of the large holdall he'd brought with him. 'I'll be here as long as it takes to see Finn through this.'

Colin McKenzie digested that information. 'Okay, just as long as you both realise he's in deep trouble.' He looked at Finn. 'If it weren't for this incident with the dog—'

'And that's the point, Sergeant,' Katie interrupted him as Finn paled all over again. 'I haven't finished with my patient yet, so I'd appreciate it if you would leave us while I tend to him.'

He nodded. 'Of course. He's all yours, Doctor. For now.'

Katie looked at the shaking boy and debated whether she ought to give him a sedative. On the other hand, he had Ross to bolster him now, and maybe that would be the boost he needed.

She wrote out a prescription for antibiotics, and

handed it to Ross. 'Could you get this filled for him? There's a late-night pharmacy on the High Street.'

'I'll do that.' He gave her a thoughtful look and said softly, 'I'll be seeing you around, Katie. Maybe you'll think some more about having dinner with me—if only as a way of letting me thank you for taking such good care of Finn.'

'Maybe,' she murmured. His fingers brushed hers as he took the prescription from her, and the brief, intimate contact sent shock waves rippling throughout her body.

Her heart was thumping, banging against her rib cage in a heavy, pounding rhythm. It was so confusing, having him here on the island, in her surgery. After all this time she'd thought she'd managed to blot him out of her mind, but here he was, back in full, whirlwind force.

How on earth was she going to cope, having him around?

CHAPTER TWO

'Isn't it great? I could hardly believe it when Maggie at the post office told me Ross McGregor is back on the island.' Jessie was bubbling with excitement, full of the news that was the talk of the village. 'I wonder if he'll decide to stay?'

'I don't think that's very likely.' Katie was listening to her sister with half an ear while she busied herself getting ready for a trip to the mainland. She'd spent the last half-hour checking her overnight bag for last-minute essentials. 'I wonder if I'll need a special dress for the evening? It's only a two-day conference after all.' She frowned, thinking it through. 'Perhaps I'll take a cocktail dress just to be on the safe side.'

'Aren't you thrilled, though, Katie?' Jessie's grey eyes were shining with enthusiasm, making her look like an excited teenager.

Katie glanced at her, holding up a simple black dress that was adorned with an embroidered pattern of silver thread at one side of the bodice. 'Excited…why? It's just a conference about using video technology for health services. There'll be a few speeches and some hands-on use of the equipment, but nothing too spectacular, I imagine. Except for the castle where it's being held, of course.' She paused to dwell on that for a moment or two. 'Now, that could be really interesting. It looks out over the loch.'

Jessie threw up her hands in a gesture of impatience. 'Honestly, Katie, you're so single-minded. Haven't you heard a word I've been saying? I'm talking about Ross— I'm so happy he's back. I've only managed to see him for a day or so each time he's been home over the last few years, but I've heard all sorts of things about him while he's been away. I wonder if he'll drop by McAskie's Bar one evening? It would be so good to meet up with him again.'

Katie laid the dress inside the bag and closed the zipper. 'I'm not so sure it would be wise to get involved with him,' she cautioned. 'You're not teenagers any more, and he could break your heart if you give him half a chance. Besides, he's only here for as long as it takes to sort out the business with Finn, and he'll walk away from us without even looking back, the same as he did before.'

'I'm not talking about getting involved with him.' Jessie shook her head, her silky black hair settling in a neat bob just below her ears. She was a beautiful young woman, with a perfect oval face, a peaches-and-cream complexion and full, well-shaped lips. She had the figure to go with all that, too. Being curvaceous and good-natured, she was every man's dream girl.

'Anyway, he didn't have much choice about leaving,' she said, her face taking on a drawn, anxious expression. 'The way things were for him at home, and with all the village against him—I don't blame him for wanting to go.'

Katie's mouth made a flat line as she thought back to that awful time. It still bothered her, all these years later, what had happened that fateful night. Ross had met up with Jessie at the Old Brewery, a secret get-to-gether, by all accounts, because her parents had made it clear they were dead set against either of their daughters seeing him.

Nothing had happened between them, Jessie had insisted afterwards—that hadn't been the intention when she'd asked him along. She'd dared him to go there with her, flouting all the rules. At fifteen, she'd been a bit wild and reckless, seeking adventure, and Ross must have seemed like the ideal partner in crime. She'd known the place was unsafe, and that had been the thrill, until it had all ended in tragedy.

Ross had suffered a terrible accident there but only after he had somehow managed to set fire to one of the outhouses.

What could have possessed him to behave in such a way that afterwards his only recourse had been to leave the village where he had grown up? There had been talk of a drifter hanging about the place, and it had been suggested that maybe he had started the fire, but no one had really believed that. Ross was the one they'd had in their sights. There had been no actual proof against him, but everyone had laid the blame at his door.

Katie still had trouble squaring it in her mind. He'd always been reckless, but causing a fire was something beyond the pale, even for him, surely?

'No,' she murmured, bringing her mind back to Jessie, 'but you know how you felt when he went away. You were devastated. You sobbed for days and moped about the house for weeks, as I recall.' Katie guessed it had probably been guilt that had made her sister react that way, but she knew that even now Jessie was impulsive, with a tendency to let her heart rule her head.

'Only because it was so tragic, him having to leave.

Besides, I was only fifteen, then.' Her sister's voice faltered and she started to flounce out of the room. 'I'm older now, and much more sensible.'

'Oh, yeah?' Katie picked up the holdall and followed her downstairs. 'I'm just saying you don't owe him anything. You don't have to make up to him for what happened in the past.' She frowned. 'I don't want to see you get hurt.'

'That's not going to happen, Katie. Ross and I are just friends, nothing more. You don't need to worry about me.'

'Well, okay, I'll try.' Katie looked around the neat, farmhouse kitchen, ticking off a list of last-minute jobs in her head. 'If the roof man phones while I'm away, will you remember to make a note of the day he'll be coming to do the work?'

'I will.'

'And try to persuade him we need the work done like…yesterday.'

'I will.'

'And don't let young Jack from next door do any weeding in the garden without supervision—he pulled up some of the aubrietia from the rockery last time I let him loose in there.'

'I won't.' Jessie laughed. 'You can trust me. I'll look after the place while you're off gallivanting.' She picked up a slice of toast left over from breakfast, slathered it with butter and bit into it. 'It's good of you to let me stay here, Katie. I thought everything was done and dusted once I'd signed the papers for my house, but I didn't realise it would take so long for everyone in the chain of buyers to move out of their own properties, or that I'd need to get my extension finished before I could move in.'

'You know I love having you here. Don't worry about it.' She glanced at her watch. 'Now, I must get a move on or I'll miss the ferry.'

'And I have to make tracks or Mum will wonder why the café hasn't been opened up, and there'll be a queue forming outside the gift shop.'

Katie gave her younger sister a hug. 'Take care. I'll be back before you know it.' Sometimes she envied her sister her simple life, working on their parents' country estate, a picturesque, rambling old house and gardens, nestled in a verdant stretch of forest, where people came to spend a day out while they soaked up the island's historic heritage.

Ross had always been conscious of the wide differences in their backgrounds, but it hadn't mattered to Katie. They'd mixed with the village children throughout their school lives, and it had seemed to her then that there were no class boundaries. They had just been children, spending their summers scrumping in the apple orchards or fishing with nets in the nearby burn.

That had been when she'd first been aware of Ross, when she'd paddled barefoot in the cool, running water and he'd shown her how to chase the fish into the shallows and then trap them in her net. He'd helped her transfer them to a jam jar filled with water, and he'd laughed when she'd insisted on tipping them back into the stream before they'd set off for home.

She shook the thoughts from her head and set off a few minutes later for the ferry port. She took the bus, looking out of the window at the beautiful wooded hills and low mountains in the distance. Soon the blue sweep of the coastline came into view, and she readied herself for the next lap of her journey.

It would be a blustery crossing, she guessed, for although the sun managed to filter through the clouds every now and again on this late August day, the wind was already stirring, lifting her hair in playful gusts.

It wasn't too long before she was standing on the deck of the ferry at last, looking out over the water. Gulls swooped and shrieked, and she smiled, relaxing against the rail as the boat began to move slowly away from port. The light breeze danced around her, pulling at the edges of her cotton jacket, adding a chill feel to her denim-clad legs.

'Well, there's a welcome surprise. My dreams have started to come true.' Out of the blue, Ross came to stand beside her, placing a hand next to hers on the rail. He smiled, looking inordinately pleased to have found her there.

'Oh!' She looked at him in startled wonder. 'What are you doing here? I thought you were planning to stay on the island for a few days?'

'I am, but I have some business on the mainland that was arranged before this happened. I was going to cancel, but Finn has perked up a bit now and his mother's being supportive, so he insisted on me going ahead with it. He doesn't have to go back to the station until the end of the week and I'll be back before then.'

'Oh, I see. Are you staying at the house with them?'

He shook his head. 'I'm renting a room at McAskie's for the time being. It's comfortable there, and the food is good, so I'm well set up.'

She guessed he didn't want to be with his father. 'It sounds as if you're doing all right, then.' Jessie would be pleased about that, at any rate. She often went to McAskie's with her friends, so she was bound to run into Ross before too long.

'And how is it that you're on board the ferry?' he asked. 'Is it a shopping trip, or are you taking a holiday?'

'Neither of those. I'm going to Loch Cragail for a medical conference.'

'Really?' A smile spread across his face, crinkling the corners of his eyes and making her heart do an unexpected flip-over. She sighed inwardly at her weakness. There was no getting away from it, he was an extraordinarily good-looking man. No wonder he was so popular with all the girls. 'I guess I get to wine and dine you after all, then,' he murmured with satisfaction in his voice. 'That's where I'm headed.'

'You're kidding.' Her jaw dropped momentarily, and he gave her a quizzical look before she recovered enough to clamp her mouth shut. How could fate conspire against her this way? Two whole days in his company? The irony of the situation struck her and she gave a wry smile. Jessie would never forgive her when she found out that she and Ross had been staying together at a luxury hotel.

'Is that such a daunting prospect? You and I could get along very well, you know, Katie,' he said in a coaxing tone, 'if you'd only give us half a chance.'

'I wouldn't bank on it.' She turned a glittering emerald gaze on him. 'I've seen you in action, remember, and I know full well that you can flit from one woman to another quite easily, without so much as a backward glance. Look what happened to poor Molly Jenkins. She fell for you, hook, line and sinker, and you left her and went off with her best friend. I've no intention of becoming one of a long line of conquests.'

His dark brows lifted. 'I'm shocked you think that way about me. In fact, it sounds almost like a challenge.' His mouth tilted a fraction. 'One I'd be more than happy to take up. But I think you're misjudging me, Katie,' he added with a frown. 'I don't set out to hurt people. Anyway, that was all a long time ago. What makes you think I'm still the same man I was then?'

'News filters through, one way or another.' She shivered a little as the wind buffeted her, and she paused to pull her jacket more closely around her. 'And you've never settled down with a woman for any length of time, have you?'

'I could say the same about you, regarding the men in your life. From what I've heard, you're very careful about whom you date, and so far I gather no one has managed to win your heart. Except maybe for one who finally got the heave-ho.'

She looked at him from under her lashes. 'It sounds as though you've been asking around.' She didn't want to talk about her ex. He'd been enough to put her off serious relationships ever since.

He grinned. 'I may have just happened to catch the odd murmur here and there, you know, as you do when people have had a drink or two. I'm always interested to hear what you've been getting up to.'

'Hmm.' She looked out over the water and shivered again as the wind began to toss her hair, sweeping silky tendrils across her cheeks. In the distance, she could see the undulating, green hills of the mainland, with whitewashed houses spread out along the coastline or clustered together in small settlements in the valleys. Behind them, mountains rose majestically, their summits shrouded in mist.

Ross reached out and lightly tucked her hair back behind her ears. 'Why don't we go to the bar and I'll buy you a drink,' he suggested. 'A brandy, perhaps, something to warm you a little?' He wrapped an arm around her waist, drawing her close.

She nodded agreement, enjoying the instant heat that came from his warm body, and they turned away from the deck rail. He kept her by his side and said in a cheerful tone, 'You can tell me all about what you've been up to these past years.'

'I've been working mostly,' she said. 'I've had to study hard to pass my specialist exams, and my job means everything to me.'

He frowned. 'So much so that you've missed out on a personal life?'

She shook her head and smiled. 'I wouldn't go as far as to say that.'

He studied her thoughtfully as they took the stairs down to the lower deck. 'You were always the sensible daughter of the family, weren't you, Katie?'

Sensible? She absorbed that comment with a rueful, inner twinge. She'd not had much choice in that, had she? When her father's angina had started giving him trouble in stressful situations, she'd made up her mind that she would do her utmost to protect him.

Jessie tried to do the same, but her nature was such that she often gave in to impulsive behaviour and only thought about the consequences afterwards.

'I've missed you,' Ross said, breaking into her thoughts. 'Whenever I've been in bother, or about to do something mad, I've had the image of your sweet, calm face before me, with your green eyes warning me not to be such a harebrained fool.' His mouth indented. 'You've a lot to answer for.'

'Oh, yes?' She gave him a doubtful look. 'I'm not sure I believe that. Since when did you ever bother about my opinion? I can't imagine you've given me much thought at all—out of sight, out of mind, isn't that what they say?'

'Such scepticism... I can see I have my work cut out with you.' There was a gleam in his eyes as he looked at her. 'Definitely a challenge.'

He led the way to the bar, still keeping his hand splayed out over the curve of her hip, sending small ripples of excitement coursing through her body, and she had to steel herself not to give in to the warm, confusing tide of emotion that ran through her at his touch.

She had mixed feelings when he left her at a table by the window to go and fetch their drinks. Part of her was relieved that she was no longer under siege to that intensely intimate and sensual onslaught, and yet another, perverse part longed once again for that delight.

'There you are,' he said a moment later, sliding a brandy glass across the table towards her. 'Drink up. You'll soon feel it warm you.'

'Thank you.' She did as he suggested, and instantly felt the heat of the alcohol suffuse her body. Idly, she looked at him over the rim of her glass, and it seemed in that moment that the intervening years fell away. He still had that youthful look about him, all that boyish charm that had melted her heart when she'd been just a teenager.

Today he was wearing dark trousers and a navy-blue shirt beneath his open jacket. The first few buttons of his shirt were undone, showing his lightly tanned throat, and she watched, as though mesmerised, as he swallowed his drink. His larynx moved, and she felt a sudden, disconcertingly intense urge to reach up and run her fingers lightly over his golden skin.

She dragged her gaze away from him. 'Do you ever look back and regret that you left the island?' she asked.

He thought about her question for a moment or two. 'In some ways, yes, for the family I left behind, but I think if I had that time all over again, I'd do the same thing. I was under a lot of pressure back then.' His eyes darkened. 'As you know, things weren't going well for me, and my father was angry and clamping down on me more than ever.'

'I know.' She took another sip of brandy, feeling the amber liquid scald the back of her throat. 'But you were badly injured, after all, and when all the hoo-hah died down after the accident, and the fire, your father might have had a change of heart. Perhaps you didn't give him the chance to see things in a different light?'

He shook his head. 'He was worried about me, I knew that, deep down, of course. But he was a stickler for doing things right and the fact was he was disappointed in me. I always seemed to be in trouble, and I guess the incident at the Old Brewery was the last straw.'

Katie nodded, understanding how things had gone so badly wrong. She didn't know the full details—only what people had said at the time, and she suspected those stories had been embellished and exaggerated. The fire had scandalised everyone, but their feelings had been tinged with sorrow because when Ross had come down from the upper storey of the old building, the rotten timbers of the staircase had given way and he had fallen to the floor below. Quite why he had gone back up there after starting the fire wasn't clear, but Katie suspected he'd gone to retrieve Jessie's jacket. She'd said she'd left it behind, and that must have added to her guilt.

Ross and Jessie had been tight-lipped about that night ever since, and neither of them wanted to talk about what had happened.

'I shouldn't have been there,' he admitted now, 'but you don't think about these things too deeply when you're young. We'd all been warned to keep away because it was abandoned and dangerous, but it drew teenagers like a magnet, and I was no exception.

'The way my father saw it, if I hadn't been there, if I hadn't acted the way I did, the accident wouldn't have happened. He was right to be angry. It was my fault for being reckless, and the fire was the last straw.'

He gave a rueful smile. 'They blamed me, and I suppose that was because my reputation for skirting the law went before me. I was unconscious, and I have no memory of it. But as far as my father was concerned it was one of a long line of misdemeanours, and I guess he was torn between anger and sorrow.'

She frowned. 'Jessie was adamant that you didn't do it.'

He nodded. 'Yes, but no one was prepared to believe her.'

It was Jessie's role that bothered Katie. She must have gone there in the first instance knowing full well her parents had forbidden it. It was a dangerous place and there were signs all around warning people to keep away, but perhaps she had simply decided to throw caution to the wind.

'You were very badly injured. It was lucky for you that Jessie was there. She must have saved your life by ringing for the emergency services.' Even now Katie tensed, thinking about what might have happened if the paramedics and fire service hadn't arrived within a few minutes of her call.

'Yes, she did.'

'You were so ill. A fractured skull—I was so worried about you. We all were.'

He reached across the table and covered her hand with his. 'I remember you came to visit me in hospital. That was like a ray of light shining down on me. It meant a lot to me, you being there, but I felt wretched knowing that you thought badly of me.'

She was startled. 'You knew I was there? But I thought... I didn't realise. I know I talked to you, but you didn't answer. You'd been in a coma. It was awful, I felt so wretched, seeing you like that, not being able to do anything.' Her voice trailed away. 'There was a time when we didn't think you would recover.'

'Well, all I can say is I must have the luck of the devil. Thanks to the surgeons I was up and about after some extensive physio and ready to do battle.' His mouth flattened. 'I knew I had to make some changes in my life after that.'

She nodded, finishing her drink. 'So did I. That's when I decided I had to study medicine. I was so impressed by the way everyone handled things, from the paramedics, the nurses, through to the doctors. It had a huge impact on me.'

He grinned. 'I'm glad I had some influence on your life in a good way. But as for myself, I knew I had to get away, to start afresh where no one had any preconceived ideas about me.'

She raised her brows. 'It was a bit drastic, though, going off and joining the army, don't you think?'

He laughed. 'Maybe.' He picked up her glass. 'Will you have another?'

'Yes, thanks. It's certainly done the trick.' While he was at the bar, she undid her jacket and slipped it off, placing it over the back of her chair. She was wearing a crocheted top over a cotton shirt blouse, and when Ross came back he gave her an admiring glance.

'You're a sight for sore eyes.'

Her mouth twitched. 'I bet you say that to all the girls.'

'Yeah. Especially those who give me the run-around. A bit of flattery goes a long way, I find.'

She laughed. 'I expect it does. You'll go far.'

'I'll drink to that.' He raised his glass and she answered the toast with hers, clinking their glasses together.

'So, here's to the future,' she murmured. 'May it bring us both what we want.'

'Mmm...I'd be more than happy to settle for you,' he returned, as quick as a flash, a light dancing in his blue eyes.

She shook her head. 'Poor, deluded man,' she said softly, swirling the amber liquid in her glass. 'Such passion...such persistence...such a waste.'

'We'll see.' He looked so confident and quietly sure of himself that she felt a momentary qualm. He wouldn't succeed, though. He was chivvying her along, playing her on a long line, but it wouldn't get him anywhere. She was immune, wasn't she? How could she fall for someone who had such a reckless nature?

She tasted the brandy once more and felt a giddying surge of heat rush to her head. She frowned. Could it be that the strong spirit was getting to her? She'd had breakfast, but that had been a while ago, and she hadn't eaten all that much then, just a bowl of cereal and a round of toast.

She started to talk, to cover her confusion. 'How was it that you turned to medicine? I meant to ask you when we met up at med school a few years ago, but we had so little time together it went out of my head.'

'Yes, I remember thinking it was almost a pity I'd

secured a place on the accident and emergency rotation. I'd hoped we could work together for a while, but you were doing paediatrics then, as I recall, and our shifts always seemed to clash.'

She nodded. 'You said the army had organised the training for you—but what was it that made you want to go in for medicine? I thought you were all set in your career with the army?'

He frowned. 'It was the general nature of the work I was doing, I think. I was in a lot of areas where there was fighting, and there were injured men being evacuated on a regular basis. The medics would come in and do what they could for the men, and then they were whisked off to hospital. I began to feel that I would like to have some part in that.

'I wanted to become a surgeon so that I could make a difference to the men who were severely wounded— I wanted to give them the chance of life. So in the end I decided to specialise in accident and emergency and neurosurgery.'

'But you left the army after all that. When did it happen?' She sipped more brandy and felt warm all over, and began to worry that she was becoming a little light-headed.

His gaze trailed over her, and she was conscious of the hot tide of colour that must be flooding her cheeks. His glance was interested and speculative at the same time. 'Only quite recently, actually. I had to stay with the army for a few years after they supported my training. I can't say I decided it was time to put down roots, exactly, but I think I'd had enough of being in conflict zones.

'It's easy to become hardened to it after a while, and I didn't like that. I didn't like what it was doing to me. I began to wonder if I could do just as much good by working in Accident and Emergency here at home.'

'I expect your father's pleased you made that decision.'

He shrugged. 'I wouldn't know. I don't see all that much of him. He's away on business a lot—he always was.' He appeared to be unperturbed by that, but there was a faint edge of regret in his voice.

After a while they finished their drinks and he said quietly, 'Shall we make our way down to the car deck? We'll be docking soon, and we might as well get ready to go.'

She gave him a quick look. 'You bought a car?'

'I hired one.' His mouth indented. 'So I'll be able to drive you to Cragail. That will make things easier for you, won't it?'

'Yes, it will. Thanks.'

She started to get to her feet and swayed slightly, so he put out a hand and helped her find her balance. 'Are you all right?'

'I'm fine, thanks.' Her brows drew together. 'I think perhaps I should have eaten more at breakfast or avoided the brandy. It seems to have gone to my head.' They walked out of the bar and along the corridor leading to the stairwell.

'I'll get you something to soak it up—a bun, a sandwich, a pack of biscuits or something,' he said. 'What would you like?'

'A bun would be great—but I can get it for myself.' She turned to walk towards the cafeteria, but he retained his hold on her, and she realised he didn't think she was steady enough to go on her own.

'Honestly, I'm all right,' she said. The dizziness

would pass soon enough, she was sure, though she was ashamed of herself for getting into this state.

'Of course you are.' A couple of passengers approached, wanting to get past them, and he tugged her gently towards him so that her soft curves were lightly crushed against his hard, masculine frame. A wave of heat raced through her body.

He pulled in a deep breath. 'You're more than all right, Katie.' He looked into her eyes and let his glance shift over the pink flush of her cheeks and down to the ripe swell of her lips. 'More tempting than you could possibly imagine. In fact, you're perfect. Delectable, and as sweet as luscious strawberries.'

And he was a charmer, a devil in disguise, who would play havoc with her feelings if she gave him half a chance. His hand smoothed over her spine, coming to rest on her hip, and despite herself she arched against him sinuously, like a cat, revelling in the gentle caress.

His smile was inviting, a small glow of satisfaction flickering in the depths of his eyes. 'I'm really glad we're going to be together at Castle Cragail,' he murmured. 'I've been longing to have you all to myself ever since we met up again at the station.'

'Hmm.' Katie wasn't so sure about that. All at once she could see all manner of pitfalls opening up in front of her. 'I'm not thinking too clearly,' she said, pushing the palms of her hands lightly against his chest, 'and I think I should take your advice and go and get something to eat. I have the feeling I need to keep a clear head.'

'What a shame,' he said softly. 'I was getting to like being with this new, befuddled Katie.'

She nodded. 'That's what I'm afraid of.'

CHAPTER THREE

THE SUN APPEARED from behind the clouds as Katie and Ross approached Cragail Castle, and Katie gave a small gasp. 'Oh, look at that, Ross—it's so beautiful. I never imagined it would be like this.'

The stonework had taken on a mellow, golden glow in the morning light, and she gazed, enraptured for a moment or two, at the circular towers and high ramparts, set against a backdrop of pine forest and green meadowland.

'We'll have to go up to the ramparts and look out over the countryside later on,' Ross murmured. 'It will have been well worth coming here just to see that.'

She smiled. 'Are you not all that interested in the conference itself?'

'I am, actually.' They walked to the main gate, passing along a stone-walled bridge that went over a bubbling stream. 'I like to keep up with all kinds of new technology—it's just that we don't always have the advantage of being in beautiful surroundings when we take part in these events.'

There was more than one conference being held at the castle, they discovered, and notice-boards had been set up in the main hall to show people where the various meetings were being held.

One of the girls from Reception showed them to their rooms, where they would be staying overnight, and Katie discovered that she and Ross had been allocated rooms on the same floor, just a few doors away from each other.

'I'll come and call for you in a few minutes,' Ross said, checking his watch. 'It looks as though we've just time to freshen up before the first meeting.'

'Okay.' Katie went into her room and laid her holdall on the softly quilted bed. There was no time to unpack so she quickly ran a brush through her hair, applied fresh lipstick to her mouth and added a touch of perfume to her throat and wrists. Then she went over to the casement window and looked out through the leaded panes over the landscaped gardens that stretched for acres in all directions. Amongst the shrubbery there was a statue half-hidden by a rose-covered archway, and a fountain where water trickled over a series of stone urns.

Ross knocked lightly on her door a moment later, and she went to meet him, ready for the day ahead.

'What's your room like?' he asked. 'Are you pleased with it?'

'It's lovely—all sunshine-yellow walls and soft furnishings,' she murmured. 'How about yours?'

'Perfect. Tartan covers and a writing table by the window. I brought my laptop with me, so that'll come in handy.'

They stayed together throughout the day, listening to various speakers talk of the advantages of video links for centres in remote rural areas, enabling doctors to link up with consultants in other parts of the region.

'I liked the idea of a new mother being able to see her baby over a video link when she had been taken to a different hospital for surgery,' Katie said, when they went to the banqueting hall to get some food a few hours later. 'It must be awful to be separated from your infant when you most want to be with him.' She surveyed the variety of dishes on offer and wondered what to choose.

Ross nodded. 'There are lots of advantages to video conferencing—it's very useful to be able to exchange ideas with other professionals, without having to travel miles to meet up with them.' He loaded his tray with steak pie and vegetables and added an apple pie for dessert. 'I'll get a pot of tea for both of us, if you like?'

She nodded, and he waved a hand towards the far side of the room. 'There's a table over there by the window. Will that be okay with you?'

'It'll be fine.' Katie chose the soup of the day, a tempting mix of appetising vegetables, and picked out a crusty bread roll to go with it. Finally, she opted for a cool fruit salad to finish things off.

She glanced around the hall as she tasted her soup a few minutes later. The oak-panelled walls were adorned with oil paintings, a mixture of local landscapes and portraits of the ancestors of the people who owned the castle.

Glittering chandeliers hung down from the ornate ceiling and high up along one side of the room she noticed a minstrels' gallery. There was no music being played at the moment, but she'd heard that in the evenings a group of musicians would gather there to provide entertainment for people who were dining.

Ross finished pouring tea and then followed her gaze. 'It looks as though a lot of care and attention has been put into this place. All the rooms have their own particular features—even the conference room was warm and welcoming. I'm not sure whether it was because of the décor or the plush seating...'

'I think it was both of those, and the flowers and greenery added the finishing touch.' She smiled. 'I suppose it would be very sexist of me to say that I think a woman has had a strong part in overseeing the interior design here.'

He grinned. 'It would but I think you're right.' He tucked into the steak pie for a while and then said on a thoughtful note, 'Did you have any particular reason for wanting to come to this conference? It's not as though you'll have much use for this technology in paediatric A and E, is it? Unless you've come across problems, of course?'

She laid down her spoon for a moment while she answered him. 'You're right—so far there hasn't been any situation where I've needed to have the equipment on hand. But I'm thinking of the wider issues. A job has come up that I'm really interested in. I felt coming here might be useful to me, because the work will involve administration—seeing to the needs of the region, not just the local hospital.'

He was silent for a moment, seemingly preoccupied with his thoughts, but then he frowned and asked, 'Are you thinking of moving away from paediatrics?'

She shook her head, making the chestnut curls gleam in the golden light of the chandelier. 'Not at all. It just means I'll have extra responsibility on top of what I'm doing now. My boss has been encouraging me to go for it. It's really important to me to get this job—I've worked hard these last few years, because I always wanted to become a consultant. This is the ideal opportunity for me to achieve that.'

'As a registrar, you're only one step away from that, though some people might think you're still rather young, and maybe you could do with a bit more experience under your belt.' His dark brows drew together. 'Is your career that important to you? What about marriage and children? Don't they figure in your plans?'

'Of course they do...at some point,' she said in a faintly troubled voice. 'But right now my job is everything to me. I love what I do.'

The truth was, there'd been boyfriends along the way, and one in particular who she'd cared about quite deeply, until she'd discovered that he'd cheated on her. That had hurt her badly, and had shaken her confidence, so that she decided to put all her energies into her work. She'd made up her mind she wasn't ever going to allow herself to be hurt that way again.

She'd learned a valuable lesson, and at the same time she'd realised that none of the men she'd dated had measured up to her ideal. Perhaps, subconsciously, she'd been setting them all against her first love...or should that be infatuation? Somehow, Ross had always been there in the back of her mind, right from the beginning. He was so wrong for her, and yet the dream had persisted. There was always that 'what if' hovering in the background.

'Katie, Ross! Who'd have thought we would meet up here?' The male voice cut into her thoughts, and Katie looked up from her seat by the window to see a tall man, immaculately dressed in a dark suit and subtly patterned silk tie, standing by their table. His dark hair had a natural wave, and his blue-grey eyes glinted with recognition.

'Josh? Josh Kilburn?' Katie smiled as she recalled the earnest young man she'd been at school with several years before. She turned to Ross, wondering if he remembered him, too.

'Hi, there,' Ross said, nodding acknowledgement.

'Are you here for the other conference—something to do with the legal profession, isn't it?'

'That's right. I'm a solicitor—we're finding out about using video links to liaise between the courts and people in prison. One way for convicts to give testimony without having to travel to and from court.'

Katie patted the chair beside her. 'Why don't you come and join us?' she suggested with a smile. 'I'd really like to hear what you've been up to these last few years.'

'I'd love to,' he said, a look of regret coming over his face, 'but I won't, thanks, because I'm with my colleagues. I just wanted to come over and say hello. I'll be staying here overnight, so if you're doing the same, perhaps we could get together at some point? I'm in room twenty-eight.'

'That must be on the floor above mine. I'm in number twelve,' Katie murmured, 'and Ross is along the corridor from me.'

'Room nine,' Ross said. 'Come and knock on the door if you want to meet up later on. Otherwise we'll be round and about the place.'

'It's great to see you again,' Katie told him. 'Are you working on the mainland? I never ventured that far—not for any length of time.'

'I was, but actually I just moved back to the village, so I guess you'll be seeing see me around from time to time. I'm a partner of a law firm setting up there.'

'That's good to know. We'll be able to catch up, and talk over old times.' She ran her gaze over him briefly. Judging by the expensively tailored suit and the crisp linen shirt he was wearing, he'd done well for himself. She could see the merest hint of gold cufflinks beneath the sleeves of his jacket. 'Will you be bringing family over with you?'

'No, just myself. I'm planning on buying a house not too far from where my parents live. It'll be good to be close to them and my brother again.' He turned as his friends tried to catch his attention. 'It looks as though they're going into the annexe to eat,' he said. 'It seems to be filling up fast in here.' He smiled. 'I'd better go. It was good meeting up with both of you—maybe we'll be able to talk again later? Perhaps we could all get together for dinner this evening?'

Katie and Ross nodded, and then, as Josh walked away, they turned their attention back to their meals.

'He used to be a regular visitor to your family estate at one time, as I recall,' Ross murmured. 'Weren't you and he dating at one time?'

'Off and on, yes, but it was nothing serious. He was always more interested in Jessie. Anyway, I left for medical school soon after.'

'How's Jessie doing? Has she left the nest or is she still working on the family estate?'

'Oh, she won't leave. She loves that job.' She sent him a wide-eyed glance. 'What's not to love—all that beautiful countryside, people wanting to be shown around the place? She's in her element there. The house is only open at certain times, though—my parents value their privacy—but there are the gardens to see, and the woodland paths, and the horse riding. I expect you know it all fairly well.'

He shook his head and looked at her from under his dark lashes. 'I was never very welcome on the estate, remember?'

She frowned, disturbed by the mixed emotions she read in his eyes. What was it she saw there? Regret? Disillusion? 'But you must have visited—Jessie brought you back to the house a few times, didn't she? I don't think I was at home then, but...'

His mouth made a wry twist. 'Your parents usually found a way to see me to the door before too long. They didn't want me around. Apparently I was a bad influence on their younger daughter.'

She sent him a concerned glance. 'I'm sorry about that. Jessie was a bit wild and headstrong in those days.' And, of course, their worst fears had come to fruition when they'd discovered Jessie had been with him that night at the Old Brewery. Perhaps that was why Jessie didn't want to talk about that incident. She knew she shouldn't have been with him, and she'd let her parents down.

His brows arced upwards. 'Didn't they have the same qualms about you? You're not much older than she is, and yet you seemed to come and go as you pleased, and as I recall you were never short of young men wanting to go out with you.'

She shrugged lightly. 'I guess they thought I was more level headed.'

'More than likely.' His blue eyes gleamed. 'You were always the one to look out for her and try to keep her out of trouble, like that night when we were all partying down by the stream, a group of us lads and some girls?'

She nodded. 'You'd set up tents. I remember being a bit shocked by that, and a tiny bit jealous. It looked such fun, but there was no way my parents would have let me join you.'

The corners of his mouth tilted. 'We were planning on sleeping out under the stars. Not that we managed to get much sleep, as I remember.'

'No,' Katie said, pushing her soup bowl to one side and starting on her fruit salad. 'Because you were all busy getting drunk on lager and vodka. There was a bottle being passed round, as I recall.'

'*Some* of them were getting drunk,' he corrected her. 'Not all of us. Anyway, I'd already told Jessie that she needed to go home before she got into trouble with her parents. I'd offered to walk her back to the estate.'

'You had?' She stared at him for a second or two, bemused, before focussing her thoughts once more. 'She didn't tell me that. All I knew was I needed to get her home before my father went on the warpath but she was having way too good a time to want to leave.'

He smiled. 'You read her the Riot Act, and she dug her heels in even further. I'm still not sure what you said to her to make her change her mind.' He gave her a quizzical look.

She coloured a little. 'I had to do something. I was worried about what would happen if my father became too stressed—his angina was starting to cause him a lot of problems, and I was afraid for him. I didn't want to see him in pain or struggling for breath, and that was almost bound to happen if he found out what Jessie was up to. I don't think she realised how bad things were for him then.'

He nodded, sympathy and understanding coming into his eyes. 'So what did you do?'

'I told her I would go home and dump her favourite clothes and all her make-up in the charity bins unless she saw sense.' She pulled a face. 'I felt terrible saying that, but I didn't see any other way out. My dad had already been looking at his watch and making veiled comments, and I'd seen him take some of his medication.'

'So it was a good thing Josh came to the rescue and offered to take her home…to take you both home,' Ross commented. 'I was annoyed with him. I was hoping you might stay with us for a while. After all, you were a couple of years older than Jessie, and I didn't think that would be a problem for you.'

She shook her head. 'I couldn't do that. For my own peace of mind I had to follow the rules of the house.' She'd wanted to, though. More than anything, she'd wanted to stay and have Ross put his arms around her and hold her close, but she'd known she couldn't, not while her father had been getting ready to come looking for them. 'Anyway, you had that roguish look in your eyes, and I didn't trust you one little bit, not with my sister, or with me.'

Even now she remembered the wrench of leaving that party. The smell of new-mown grass had been in the air, there had been a lot of laughter and some of the gang had paired up, so there had been a few couples kissing in the moonlight, while others had been dancing to the music from a portable stereo. The temptation of spending time with Ross had been almost more than she'd been able to handle.

'Mmm. So Josh and I walked you both home. I remember consoling myself with the thought that there would be other times when I might persuade you to sample forbidden fruit.' His mouth curved as he watched her, a wicked gleam flickering in the depths of his eyes. 'And I was right, wasn't I?'

'I don't want to talk about that,' she said, taking refuge in hiding behind her teacup and watching him over the rim. He was right, of course. There'd been another night, another party, when Jessie had been away on a weekend break with a friend's family, and *she* had been given permission to sleep over at a friend's house. Only the birthday celebration that had started out so naively in intent had slipped into something far more intimate, as far as she had been concerned.

The lights had been dimmed, and she had found herself in Ross's arms, where all thoughts of being her natural, sweet and innocent self had gone straight out of the window. She'd wanted him with an intensity that had made her whole body tremble, and it had only been when her friend's parents had returned from their night out that sanity had returned. How close she'd come to offering up her body to him had shocked her to the core.

He chuckled. 'Okay. My lips are sealed. It just struck me that some other young man was after you that night, too. His loss was my gain.'

Her emerald eyes narrowed on him, and he held up his hands in mock surrender. 'I'm done. I promise.' He closed his mouth and made a zipping motion with his fingers across his lips.

Katie put her cup down. 'I think it's time we headed back to the conference room, don't you?' she said.

'Or we could play truant instead,' he suggested with a glint in his eye, and she aimed a light backhanded slap at his arm.

'Behave yourself,' she muttered. 'Heaven help us, we've another day to get through after this.'

They walked back to the conference room, and sat through the rest of the presentations. Katie tried not to be aware of Ross, sitting beside her, his thigh lightly brushing her own, but she was fighting a losing battle.

Eventually, he stretched, easing his taut limbs as the talks came to an end and people started making their way out of the large hall. 'Shall we meet up in, say, an hour, and take a walk in the grounds for a while before dinner?' he suggested, as they headed back to their rooms.

'Yes, that would be good. Perhaps you should make it a couple of hours. That should give me time to shower and change.'

'All right. I'll come and call for you at seven-thirty.' He waited as she let herself into her room, and then walked away down the corridor.

Katie shut the door behind her and went to sit on the soft bed for a while. There was plenty of time to get ready. She would relax for a while and read the beginning of the book she had downloaded on to her e-reader. And then she must check her emails to see if the human resources department had received her application for the post of consultant/administrator. There was plenty of time to do all that.

She switched on the small computer and idly flicked through the pages of the book. Sunlight slanted in through the leaded windowpanes and after a while the words began to shift about and blend into one another and her eyelids began to weigh heavy. It wouldn't hurt to close them for a second or two, would it? It had been such a long day, and she'd been up late last night, helping Jessie sort out the problems she was having with the extension to her house. They would have to keep a close eye on the building work…

She woke with a start an hour and a half later, when the alarm on the laptop started to bleep a low-battery warning. She looked around, dazed for a moment, wondering where she was, and then, as she glanced at her watch, sprang into confused action.

A quick shower, then put on her make-up. She would have to forgo washing her hair. Would it be okay? She ran a hand through it. It was still soft and silky—it would be fine. She laid out her black dress on the bed, grabbed fresh underwear and hurried into the bathroom.

The hot water revived her, making her feel fresh and ready for the evening ahead, though she discovered to her dismay that the steam in the bathroom had made her curls springier than ever. As she towelled herself dry, she saw her reflection in the mirror and realised there was a wild, untamed look about her. There was no way she'd be able to comb her hair into place in the time she had left.

She put on clean underwear and then opened the window a fraction to let out the steam. What time was it? She laid her damp towels over the rail and padded, barefoot, into the bedroom, closing the door behind her.

The maid had been in and left clean towels on the bed while she had been in the shower, and Katie smiled. Everything about this place was so good, well organised and catered to the guests' comfort.

'Uh…I…' From across the room, Ross coughed, and Katie spun round, startled to see that he was standing by the window, looking at her with an arrested expression in his eyes. She stared back at him in stunned surprise, and he said in a roughened voice, 'I…uh…the maid saw me knocking at the door and let me in… I'd no idea you'd be…um…' His mouth tilted at the corners. 'Wow…what can I say?'

Belatedly, she pressed an arm to her lace-covered breasts and draped the other one awkwardly across her briefs. 'She let you in? I didn't… I mean… I fell asleep. I shouldn't have… I… It was Jessie…we were up very late and I…um…'

She sucked in a deep breath. 'I should get dressed,' she said, backing up towards the bed.

He nodded. 'Yes, I suppose you must, but…' A ragged groan rumbled in his throat. 'You look lovely, Katie.' His gaze drifted over her as though he couldn't bear to drag it away. 'You take my breath away. It seems such a shame to cover up such a beautiful body.'

Katie stared at him, her green eyes wide, her lips parting a fraction. He thought she looked good? That gave her a warm glow that radiated all the way from her abdomen up to the very roots of her hair. Her whole body tingled in response to the searing lick of his gaze.

Returning that glance, she realised he didn't look so bad himself. A tall, strong man, his features were hewn by the tough years he'd spent in the army, when he'd been helicoptered into troublespots all over the world. He was a man who could take care of his woman. He would protect her, keep her safe from all comers—but not from himself, a small inner voice warned.

He had started to come towards her, slowly, thoughtfully, giving her ample time to move away, and she knew exactly how much of a risk she was taking by standing still.

And yet she couldn't bring herself to retreat. She wanted him to come near her. She wanted to feel his arms around her, to feel her body next to his, and he certainly wasn't going to disappoint her. He drew her to him, his hot, dark gaze meshing with hers, and she was instantly lost, caught up in a swirl of chaotic emotions, her feminine curves crushed by his long, tautly muscled frame, his powerful thighs pressuring hers.

He bent his head, taking her mouth in a sweet, lingering possession, tasting her, slowly exploring the softness of her lips. Her arms curved up around his neck, her fingers tangling in the silky hair at his nape, while her body revelled in the heady sensation of his stroking hands seeking out the feminine contours of her hips, her waist, the smooth line of her thigh.

And then he gently nuzzled the soft skin of her throat,

the creamy slope of her shoulder, and murmured raggedly, 'Mmm. You smell so good, Katie. So perfect. You're intoxicating.' His hand lightly cupped the firm swell of her breast and she gasped, a soft sigh that hovered on her lips as his fingers began to gently trace the lacy edge of her bra.

Sensation piled on sensation as his expert hands caressed her, making her want what she should not have, making her long for something more, and then with one slick, breathtaking movement he reached behind her and unhooked the clasp of her bra.

Only then did she know a faint qualm of anxiety. Ought she to stop this here and now before things ultimately got out of hand? If they made love, where did it leave things between them? It was so hard to think straight while he was holding her like this.

She needed him, yearned to feel his hard body next to hers without the hindrance of clothes, but she knew there would be no going back from this point. She would lose herself in him and then, when he walked away, back to his home here on the mainland, she would mourn his loss as though it was a bereavement. Would he even look back and wonder how she was doing?

There was a knock at the door and she stiffened at the unwelcome intrusion. Who could it be—more hotel staff?

She looked up into Ross's eyes, and he kissed her swiftly, a hard, demanding, achingly wonderful kiss, but a brief one also as she gently laid her hands on his chest.

'Ross, the door, someone's there.'

'Ignore it,' he murmured huskily, frustrated by the distraction and eager to get back to that blissful state of mutual passion.

'We can't,' she whispered. 'If it's the staff, they'll use their room key if we don't answer.'

'I'll tell whoever it is to go away.' His arms circled her warmly, but she wriggled, easing herself away from him.

'No.' She hesitated, then said slowly, 'I think it's for the best that this happened. I should never have let things get this far. I've been hurt before, Ross, and I don't want to go there again.'

'Katie, are you in there?' The knocking came again. 'It's Josh. I called on Ross, but he isn't in his room.'

The breath caught in her throat. It was as though fate had stepped in and made the decision for her. 'I'll go and get dressed,' she whispered. 'Wait until I'm in the bathroom and then let him in.'

Ross's expression was anguished, as though he was in some kind of physical pain, but he must have seen that she was determined and he reluctantly eased himself away from her a fraction. 'I wouldn't hurt you, Katie,' he said, in a choked voice. 'Believe me.'

'Even so.' She began to draw away from him. After all, he'd say anything she wanted to hear right now, wouldn't he?

'If that's what you really want.' His eyes darkened, becoming smoky with heat, urging her to change her mind.

'It is. I'm sorry.'

He relinquished his hold on her, and she quickly turned away from him and went to pick up her dress from the bed. Pausing only to get her make-up bag from the dressing table, she fled to the bathroom.

A moment later, she heard Ross open the door. 'Hi,' he said in an even tone. 'Come in, Josh. Katie's getting ready. You know how women are. They take an age to put on their make-up.'

She didn't hear Josh's reply. By, then, she was too busy trying to control her breathing and telling herself that she'd had a lucky escape. She couldn't give in to temptation. She wouldn't let herself be hurt again, and that was bound to happen if she let herself fall for Ross, wasn't it?

He was wrong for her in every way, and she'd meant it when she'd said she wouldn't become just one more conquest. Being with him meant far too much to her. She needed it to be special between them, and there was no way that could happen. He would never commit to any woman.

He was an opportunist, and it was his good fortune that she'd happened to fall into his hands just now like a ripe fruit.

From here on she would have to be much more careful. There was just a week or so before he had to come back to his home here on the mainland—surely she could hold out for that short length of time?

CHAPTER FOUR

'IT SOUNDS AS though the conference went well.' The triage nurse checked their small patient's notes and dropped the file back in the wire tray. She was a pretty young woman, with fair hair pulled back into a ponytail and bright, all-seeing blue eyes. 'It's probably a good thing you went along and gathered all that information. The boss was certainly pleased, anyway.'

'It'll be more to the point if management decides to put any of my ideas into practice,' Katie murmured, 'but I suppose I'll have to get this new job if I want to see that happen.' She glanced at the whiteboard where details of patients being treated or awaiting treatment were listed. 'There's no let-up today, is there? It's as though children are having a last fling before they go back to school, and all kinds of accidents are happening.'

'There's been nothing too bad so far,' Shona said, and then clapped a hand to her mouth as Katie sent her a mock-horrified look.

'Are you inviting trouble?' Katie asked. 'You know what happens as soon as someone says that. Just wait for the siren to start howling.'

'Och! I can't think what's the matter with me. It must be that lovely Ross McGregor who has put me in all of a dither. I've not been myself since I set eyes on him in the staffroom a wee while back.'

Katie's brows shot up. 'You mean he's here, at the hospital? How has that come about? What's he doing here?'

Shona shrugged. 'I don't know the ins and outs of it, only that he's been chatting to all the folk he knows from way back. Perhaps he's just come in for a while to renew old acquaintances. He can come and talk to me any time. I'm more than happy to spend time with him.'

Katie gave a wry smile. 'Not you as well? Ross always did know how to charm the ladies...' She frowned. 'Yes, it could be that he's just dropped by to say hello, I suppose.' After what had happened between them at the castle, though, she'd hoped she might avoid him for a while, but it seemed her luck was out.

But to have him here, now...it was too soon. When she'd finally dressed and put on her make-up that night, she'd wondered if things might calm down a fraction, and they could go back to being simply friends and colleagues, but it had been a vain hope. He'd devoured her with his eyes when she'd stepped back into the room, and suddenly she'd been conscious of every rounded curve she possessed, where the black dress had clung faithfully to her body.

It hadn't helped that Josh had been attentive towards her, too, albeit only in a friendly, easygoing manner. But Ross had clearly decided he wasn't going to give Josh the slightest chance to muscle in and, to her shame, that knowledge invigorated her. It had been clear he wanted her, and she had suddenly felt heady with a secret sense of power—only, she'd known she was playing with fire. Ross's hot gaze had told her that every time she'd glanced his way.

But it wouldn't do. It wouldn't work between them—she needed someone steady and reliable, and from what she knew of Ross, he wasn't that man. She needed time to put him out of her mind.

'You go for your interview this afternoon, don't you?' Shona said, switching on the light box and looking at an X-ray film. 'Hmm, that looks like a fracture to me,' she murmured. 'Am I right?'

'Yes, my appointment's first thing after lunch. And, yes, it's a fracture. It's a fairly straightforward one, so we'll reduce it under anaesthetic and then send the child to the plaster room.'

Shona nodded. 'I'll go and get him ready. He's been given painkillers so he shouldn't be too unsettled. Will you be along in a minute or two?'

'I will. I just need to check on a patient in bay three.'

By the time she'd dealt with both patients, the phone started to ring, and she knew with a sixth sense that it meant trouble was on the way.

'A baby is coming in by ambulance,' Shona said. 'He's just three weeks old, poor mite, suffering from a racing heart, unusual sleepiness and reflux vomiting. His GP has been treating him for congestive heart failure. He'll be here in ten minutes. His records are being faxed through.'

'Okay, let's get ready to receive him.' As she glanced across the room Katie saw that Ross had come into the triage area, and her heartbeat quickened in response. She had no idea how long he'd been standing there.

He was wearing pristine, dark grey trousers, teamed with a deep blue shirt and silver-grey tie, and she could see straight away why all the women drooled over him. Long limbed, flat stomached, he was strength and masculinity and cool confidence all rolled into one.

'Would it be all right with you if I come and observe?' he asked. 'I heard what Shona was saying and I'd be really interested to see what goes on.' He came to stand by the desk, and Katie sent him a quick, thoughtful glance. 'I won't get in your way,' he promised.

She nodded. 'I heard you were here. I expect it's been good for you to meet up with old friends—you know quite a lot of the staff, I gather?'

'I do. I've spent a pleasant morning looking around, catching up, but if there's any way I can be useful here, let me know. Your boss is okay with me helping out, and I'm free for a few hours. I know you're run off your feet today with a lot of the staff away on vacation or off sick.'

'All right. But if you really mean it, you'll need to put on some scrubs. I have to go to the ambulance bay.'

He smiled. 'I'll be booted and suited before you know it.'

The tiny baby was quickly wheeled into the resuscitation room, where Katie did a swift examination. 'The veins in his neck are pulsing,' she told Ross, who appeared at her side just as she was running a stethoscope over the infant's chest. It was a bad sign, and she was concerned as she listened to his heartbeat and to the sound of his lungs. She handed the stethoscope over to Ross, so that he could confirm her diagnosis.

'Congestive heart failure,' he said, with a worried frown. 'Poor little fellow. We need to find out what's going on here. What do his notes say?'

Just then the baby began to convulse, and Katie had to act quickly, injecting him with an anti-epileptic medication. A short time later, when the seizure began to recede, she stroked the downy skin of the infant's cheek and said softly, 'His doctor says he was diagnosed with a malformation of the vein of Galen in his brain. The consensus was that they didn't want to operate on such a tiny baby, but then his heart started to fail and they tried to control the situation with medication. Unfortunately, it hasn't worked.' She pulled a face. 'The outlook doesn't look good, does it?'

Ross shook his head. The baby was struggling to breathe, and Katie carefully put a tube down his throat so that he could be given life-saving oxygen.

'What do you plan to do?'

'A cranial ultrasound to begin with, just to check the original diagnosis.' She turned to Shona. 'We'd better do an ECG, and a cardiac echo, too. Will you reassure the parents that we're doing everything possible to find out all we can about Sam's illness? Give them coffee, or tea, or whatever, and help them to feel comfortable while they're waiting.'

'I will. I'll set up the ECG first.'

'Thanks.' In the meantime, Katie programmed the ultrasound machine and carefully moved the transducer probe over the infant's head. The machine was connected to a monitor, and Ross frowned as the images began to show on the screen.

'There's definitely a vein malformation,' he said.

Katie nodded. 'Let's get an MRI scan and find out exactly what we're dealing with here. Things might have changed in the last couple of weeks.'

The MRI scan only confirmed her worries. 'It's a very rare type of aneurysm,' she said, studying the films. 'We can't rely on medication to stabilise his condition, and I think he needs an immediate embolisation. The problem is that there aren't that many neurosurgeons who can do this type of work. Certainly there's no one at this hospital who would be able to do it.' She frowned, thinking it through. 'I'll make some enquiries. In the meantime, we'll have to get a cardiologist to manage the heart failure.'

'As you say, I don't think we can wait more than a few hours,' Ross put in, 'otherwise his outcome will be very poor. At the very least, he could suffer brain damage and organ failure, and at worst he might die.'

Katie nodded agreement. The blood vessels carrying nutrients to the brain had short-circuited, and were going via another route to the heart, causing it to pump faster in order to get blood and oxygen to the brain. The heart was overloaded with stress, and this tiny baby's chances weren't good at all.

'I'll go and make those phone calls,' she said. 'Will you take him back to Resus for me?'

'I will.'

When she had finished making her calls and arrived back in Resus, the news wasn't any better. 'There are two specialists who could do the surgery, but they're both out of the country right now. By the time either one of them manages to get back here, it will probably be too late. And our paediatric neurosurgeons are both in surgery, working on emergencies. We have locums here because of the holiday season, but they're not skilled in this type of surgery.'

Ross pulled in a deep breath. 'Perhaps I could help,' he offered. 'I've specialised in neurosurgery, and I trained intensively in paediatric neurosurgery quite recently when I left the army.'

She lifted a brow. 'That's a huge change of direction for you, isn't it, from adult surgery to paediatrics?'

He shrugged. 'I wanted to do something different, yet allied to what I'd been doing before. It's always been in my mind that some youngsters suffer nasty accidents the way I did, way back, and I wanted to be able to do something about it—kind of to repay the surgeons for what they did for me, you know?'

She smiled, touched by his sensitivity. 'Yes, I think I understand. But as to operating on Sam, this kind of surgery is highly unusual—this particular type of malformation is only seen around half a dozen times a year in this country.'

'Yes—which is why I'm thinking that if we could rig up some kind of video link with one or both of the surgeons who are out of the country, they could perhaps talk me through the procedure. Couldn't we get the technicians to work on that—if the doctors are agreeable to it, of course?'

Katie studied him, anxious and uplifted at the same time. She knew Ross well enough to know he was always up for a challenge, but he wouldn't take undue risks where a child's life was concerned, would he?

'Are you sure about this?'

He nodded. 'Quite sure.'

She thought about it for a moment or two. 'Okay,' she said. 'I'll have a word with my boss. If Mr Haskins is happy to let you go ahead, we'll see what we can do, and hope that we can get young Sam prepped for surgery this morning.'

A short time later Katie asked Shona to go and talk to the parents once more. 'We'll need them to fill in a consent form.'

'Does that mean we're on?' Ross glanced at her, his whole body energised and alert.

'It does. Apparently Mr Haskins has heard great things about you and one of the surgeons has agreed to stand by for the video link. We have a technician here who will help set things up.' Katie gave him a quick smile. 'Do you want to go and talk the parents through the procedure, and explain to them what's happening? And then you should go and scrub up. I'll see you in Theatre in an hour.'

'Okay. I'll introduce myself to them.' He went with Shona to the waiting room.

An hour later, the full team was assembled in the radiology suite, where little Sam was being made ready for the surgery. He looked so frail, his tiny limbs twitching occasionally, his chest rising and falling rapidly. His lips had taken on a faintly blue tinge.

Katie gently stroked his dimpled fingers. She wanted to pick him up and cradle him in her arms and whisper soothingly that everything would be all right, but she couldn't, of course, and that made her terribly sad.

The anaesthetist started to introduce the drugs that would put the baby out, and once that was done, the way was open for Ross to begin. From this moment everything depended on him and whether he had the skill to do what was needed.

He appeared to be totally calm. 'Okay, shall we get started?' He inserted a needle into a blood vessel in the baby's groin, and then slowly, carefully, pushed a soft guide wire along the blood vessel. Then he removed the needle and threaded a narrow plastic tube over the wire, feeding it through the blood vessels until he reached the malformation deep within the base of Sam's brain.

All the while, he kept glancing at the monitor that showed him how the tube was progressing. On the video link, Professor Markham intervened every now and again to make sure that all was going well.

'That's in position.' Ross murmured. 'Now I'm going to block some of the feeder arteries.'

Katie marvelled at how composed he was as he injected a glue-like substance into the malformation. She'd never seen him quite like this before, cool, confident, totally dedicated. He completed that part of the procedure and then stretched, easing his tight muscles, and she felt a compelling urge to go over to him and gently massage his neck and shoulders. It irked her that she had to restrain herself.

They had been in this room for nearly two and a half hours, and everyone was under considerable strain. The tension in the room was almost palpable. So much depended on getting this right.

'That seems to be working,' Professor Markham commented, after a while. 'The blood flow is decreasing through the lesion, and his heart rate is improving. I think you might have done it.'

'We did it between us,' Ross murmured. 'I couldn't have done it without the whole team.' He looked around. 'Thanks, everyone. Let's finish up here, shall we?'

Katie breathed a sigh of relief, along with everyone in the room. Already Sam's skin was pinking up, and on the monitor she could see that the blood had diverted along the right track.

'That was brilliant,' she told Ross later as they tossed their scrubs into a bin and cleaned up at the washbasins. 'I was afraid it would all go wrong, but you did so well. You saved that baby's life.'

'Like I said, it was down to teamwork. The professor was there to guide me through it, and everyone in the room was highly skilled and knew exactly what they had to do. I'm just pleased that the baby has a good chance in life now.'

He dried his hands and sent her an oblique glance. 'I'll go and talk to the parents, but after that, maybe we could go and get some lunch? You must be due for a break by now?'

'Yes, that's a good idea. They do a decent meal selection in the restaurant here.' She gave a wry grin. 'Not quite up to the standard of Cragail, I'm afraid, but pretty good all the same.'

'Ah, well, Cragail was an outstanding experience in more ways than one.' A mischievous gleam danced in his eyes, and Katie felt her cheeks grow warm.

'Maybe we should try to put that behind us.' She walked to the door and he stood to one side and opened it for her.

He gave her a rueful smile. 'That's more easily said than done.' He frowned, giving her a questioning look. 'I'd really like to know more about this man who hurt you.'

'It's in the past, over and done with, and I'd sooner not talk about it,' she muttered.

'Hmm. It still feels raw, does it?'

She didn't answer him, and instead they walked in silence along the corridor to the restaurant. It was light and welcoming, with clean magnolia-painted walls and wide windows overlooking a shrubbery and grassed area. To one side of the landscaped garden there was a terrace laid out with bench tables and dotted about with tubs of flowers.

'Shall we go and sit outside?' Ross suggested as they loaded their trays with food. 'It's a beautiful day. We might as well enjoy the sunshine while we can.'

'Okay.'

Katie chose a table in a secluded corner close by the shade of a gnarled sycamore tree. She had picked out an appetising and colourful cheese salad for her meal, whilst Ross had opted for lasagne. Neither of them had wanted a hot drink, and instead they had taken bottles of cola and juice from the fridge.

Ross poured juice into a glass and slid it across the table towards her. 'You were very capable and in control of everything back there in Accident and Emergency this morning,' he said. 'I was impressed. You handled the staff well, you were good with the parents, and very gentle and compassionate with the children in your care.'

She arched her brows in surprise. 'I'd no idea you saw me with anyone other than little Sam.'

'Oh, yes. I was wandering around the treatment bays earlier this morning. Mr Haskins suggested I take a look around. I didn't want to disturb you because you were busy.'

'How does our hospital compare with yours over on the mainland?'

'It's very much on a par with what we have. Of course, there's the isolation factor here and the lack of highly specialised equipment. There's always the possibility that a patient might have to be sent over to us.'

'Is that why you prefer being on the mainland, because of the state-of-the-art hospitals?'

He shrugged. 'There are pros and cons. I've pretty much learned how to be adaptable over the years.'

'And how are you finding things over here? Are you still staying at McAskie's?'

'Yes, I'm comfortable there.' He grinned. 'The landlady's taken me under her wing and makes sure I have everything I need.'

Katie rolled her eyes. Yet another woman had fallen under his spell. She'd no doubt he knew the effect he had on women and was amused by it.

She tasted her grated cheese and crisp salad then sipped the refreshing, chilled orange juice. 'Haven't you thought about going home to stay with your father and Finn for a while?'

He shook his head, becoming serious. 'I'd like to see more of Finn, but I prefer to meet him away from the house. You know my father and I don't see eye to eye. We haven't done in years.'

'Not since he married your stepmother, in fact. Isn't that the truth? It wasn't just your delinquent behaviour and the accident that caused the problems between you, was it? Those problems started because of the marriage.'

His eyes darkened. 'You were always far too perceptive.' His pressed his lips into a taut, flat line. 'It seemed to me my mother hadn't long died, and yet he brought Stephanie home. I must have been about twelve at the time, but even then I felt it wasn't right. I loved my mother to bits and I was devastated when she died.'

'I'm so sorry, Ross." She reached across the table and laid her hand lightly on his. 'It must have been an awful time for you. I can only imagine how you must have felt.'

He acknowledged her sympathetic gesture with a faint nod. 'I don't know how he could have done what he did. I didn't want anyone to take my mother's place. She was so precious to me, and it was so hard to bear when she had gone. I only knew grief at the time, but afterwards, years later, I think it made me feel closed in, and afraid to ever feel such love again, just in case…' He broke off, and Katie glanced at him, concerned by the dark torment in his eyes.

'In case you were to be hurt again?' Her heart went out to him. It explained such a lot about why he found it so difficult to make a commitment to any one woman.

He nodded. 'I think I hated my father for bringing another woman into the house.'

'That's understandable.' Katie pulled in a quick breath. 'Look, I know I may be stepping out of line here, but that all happened a long time ago, and things have changed. Don't you think it's time you and he buried the hatchet?'

He shook his head. 'I don't think that's possible. After all, we never really got on. I felt he was too harsh, too rigid in his ways, and too shut away from family life. He spent a lot of time away on business while I was growing up, and I don't believe he's changed much in these last few years.'

'He might have mellowed with age. Isn't that possible?'

'Maybe. But Finn has been telling me that he wants to leave home as soon as he can find a way to support himself. It's almost impossible to live up to my father's standards and if you fail in any way you tend to suffer for it. He's a hard man to live with in many ways, though one thing I will say for him—he was always good to my mother, and he adores Stephanie.'

'I'm sorry. I know it must have been difficult, both for you and for Finn. But you're not a boy any more, Ross, and it seems such a shame that you and your father are still at odds with one another. Now that you're older, you could perhaps reason with him and help him to see how his actions are driving Finn away.'

'I'm sure I don't need to tell my father anything about his character.' His jaw was rigid. 'He's had years to hone it to perfection, and I'd as soon leave him to get on with it.' He shot her a quick glance. 'You really don't need to worry about our relationship.'

She studied him thoughtfully. 'You're right, it's not my business, and perhaps I shouldn't try to meddle, but I just hate to see you and your father on opposite sides. It could be that deep down inside he has regrets, too.' She hesitated. 'I can see you're annoyed with me, though, and I'm sorry for that.'

'No, I'm not annoyed with you.' He laid down his knife and fork with a small sigh. 'I could never be at odds with you. My only worry is for Finn. I'll just be glad if I can help him out in any way.'

'He has to report for questioning at the police station in a few days, doesn't he? Have you found a solicitor to act for him yet?'

'I think so.' He took a long swallow of his drink. 'I made enquiries and picked out a firm that deals with juvenile crime. They're going to send someone along to talk to him.'

'Good.' She toyed with her dessert, a creamy mousse that was chilled to perfection. 'How are his wounds healing? Do you know if he's been along to the surgery to have his dressing changed?'

He nodded. 'They won't take the stitches out for a while yet, but the nurse seemed to think it was looking clean and good. You did a neat job there.'

She smiled. 'I tried. After all, youngsters are very sensitive about their looks, aren't they?'

'True.' He glanced at her, his gaze skimming over her from head to toe. 'While we're on the subject, you're looking pretty good yourself. Is that how you usually dress for work? It must make things really difficult for the male staff around here. They must have trouble concentrating. I'm really very jealous that they get to be near you.'

'Yeah, yeah.' She wafted his comments away. 'I'm sure they cope.' She was wearing a pencil skirt along with a soft-textured white blouse, and there was a jacket that nipped in at the waist to complete the outfit.

He smiled. 'Seriously, you look terrific, but don't you find that slim-line skirt a bit restricting for work?'

She shook her head. 'I usually wear scrubs when I'm in A and E, or something cheerful when I'm on the paediatric ward, but I changed into this outfit after we finished in Theatre. I don't have to work this afternoon. I have an appointment to attend in half an hour, so I need to look smart.'

'Well, you certainly look it.'

'Thanks.' She returned his gaze. 'You look well turned out, too, but I expect you always dress like that for work, don't you?' She noticed his jacket was carefully placed over the back of his seat. 'Most doctors here wear tailored trousers and a shirt and tie, though a lot of them roll up their sleeves and lose the tie for hygiene reasons these days when they're in the treatment areas.'

'It's true, we're expected to look the part—professional, well turned out, but...' He hesitated a little and she wondered if he was troubled by what he was about to say. He seemed to brace himself. 'I have an appointment, too, this afternoon. I have to be in the executive director's office at three o'clock.' He studied her, as though waiting for her reaction.

A small gasp hovered on her lips. 'You're going for an interview?' she said in a shocked voice.

He nodded, watching her cautiously, his expression serious. 'That's right.'

Her jaw dropped a fraction and she felt as though all the air had been sucked out of her, leaving her floundering. 'So that's why you've been hanging about all morning. You weren't here to renew old acquaintances at all—you were looking around, eyeing up the facilities and checking out the way we work, getting ready for any questions that might come your way this afternoon.'

She felt sick with disappointment. 'We're in competition for the same job.'

She'd had no idea this was coming. How could he have kept it to himself? 'You knew this was the job I wanted. You must have known when we were at the castle. Why didn't you tell me?'

He gave her a rueful glance. 'I didn't want to throw you off your stride or do anything to spoil things between us.'

'No, of course not,' she said in a bitter tone, 'you were too intent on trying to get me into bed, weren't you? Telling me about the job would have put a real dampener on that, wouldn't it?'

'It wasn't like that, Katie.'

"No?' She was scornful. 'I wonder why I don't believe you.'

'I don't want to argue with you, Katie.' He straightened his shoulders and added briskly, 'Anyway, it shouldn't be a problem. You have just as much chance of getting this job as I do. More, perhaps, because you already work here.'

'We'll soon see, won't we?' She stood up, pushing her chair back and reaching for her handbag. All at once she needed to escape, she desperately needed time to get herself back under control. 'I must go and freshen up. I expect I'll see you around.'

He got to his feet, his eyes narrowing on her as she turned away. 'Katie, don't let this mess things up for us,' he said tautly. 'It doesn't have to be a problem, you know.'

She didn't answer him. It was too late for those kinds of sentiments. He hadn't told her that he had applied for the job, and that hurt badly. It was such a shock.

CHAPTER FIVE

'HOW'S THE PATIENT doing, Doctor? Do we need to send him to the hospital, or will you be able to treat him here?' Sergeant McKenzie finished writing up the charge sheet and looked at Katie over the counter.

'I'm afraid we need to get an X-ray of his hand,' she told him. 'When he smashed his fist into the wall, he not only caused a lot of surface damage but it looks as though he broke a couple of fingers, too. I've cleaned it up and bound the hand to make it more comfortable for him in the meantime. He needs to keep it in the sling for now. And I've given him painkillers. They should keep on working for the next few hours.'

'Thanks, Katie. I'll organise transport and arrange for a couple of officers to escort him to the hospital.' He picked up the phone and made the arrangements there and then, while Katie chatted with the policeman who had brought the man into the station.

She turned, though, as the main door opened once more, and her chest tightened as Ross walked into the reception area, accompanied by Finn. Following them, she was surprised to see Josh Kilburn, dressed flaw-lessly as usual and carrying a bulging briefcase.

'Hi, there.' She acknowledged both men with a quick nod, and immediately struggled with the vision of Ross's powerfully honed, muscular frame. He was wearing chinos and a loose sweater that drew her attention to his broad shoulders. She looked away. She wouldn't let him distract her.

She was still annoyed with him. He must have known all along that they were going after the same job, yet he had said nothing to her about it. Heavens, he might even have managed to manoeuvre her into bed with him if they hadn't been interrupted.

She closed her eyes briefly, as though that would shut out those unsettling thoughts. After a second or two, though, she pulled herself together and managed to give Finn a warm smile. 'How are you doing, Finn?'

'I'm all right, I guess,' he answered in a hesitant voice. Bending his head towards her, he added quietly, 'I'm a bit nervous, to be honest.'

She gave his arm an affectionate squeeze. 'You're bound to be apprehensive. Let Mr Kilburn guide you. I expect he's already talked to you about what happened, hasn't he?'

'Yes. He's going to try and get the police to drop the charges.' He glanced at the sergeant, who was talking to Ross. 'I'm sure he still won't believe me, though, when I say I wasn't with the gang.'

'Just keep on telling the truth, Finn. It's important you do that.' She glanced at the dressing on his ear. 'I was glad to hear that you're having that checked regularly. It's important to keep the wound absolutely clean and dry, you know.'

He nodded, shifting restlessly from one foot to the other and curling and uncurling his fingers as though he didn't quite know what to do with himself.

'How's your mother?' she asked, trying to take his

mind off things. 'You said she'd been ill with a virus recently. Is she still poorly?'

'Actually, she seems a little bit better in herself. She's started to eat a bit more, but she's lost weight and she still gets tired very easily. I tell her to rest, and I try to help, but she looks worn out all the time.'

Katie frowned. 'If she hasn't been eating properly for quite a while, it's possible she could be short on iron. Try to persuade her to go and see her doctor to get her iron levels checked. It might be that she needs a vitamin and mineral supplement.'

'I will. Thanks, Katie.'

'You're welcome, Finn.'

'All right, then, lad, it's time for you to come along with me to the interview room.' Sergeant McKenzie waved a hand towards the corridor, and Finn straightened up and reluctantly followed him. Josh stayed by his side as they walked along.

Ross didn't immediately go after them, but instead stayed behind to send Katie a quizzical glance. 'Are you still mad at me about the interview?' he asked in a low voice.

She lifted her chin and returned his gaze. 'I think we both know the answer to that,' she said tersely.

'I didn't know you were going after the job when I sent in my application, Katie. But you knew you would be up against competition, didn't you?'

'Of course. I just expected you to be straight with me about it.'

'Yes, well...' He hesitated. 'Perhaps we'll find time to talk later.' It was clear he wasn't happy with her answer, or the way she'd said it, but he was obviously conscious that he needed to be at Finn's side. After a moment's hesitation he reluctantly turned to go with the others to the interview room.

Katie went back into her surgery and prepared to hand over her patient to the police escort. 'I've written up a treatment card for you to hand in at A and E,' she told the man. 'They'll want to X-ray the hand and wrist to see what damage has been done. I'm sure you'll be well looked after.'

'Thanks.' He mumbled the word and appeared resigned to spending time in A and E. She guessed by now he was regretting his impulsive action.

The two young policemen stepped forward. 'Are we all done here, Doctor?' the older one asked, and Katie nodded.

'He's all yours.'

They left the station, and Katie tidied the room before writing up her notes on the computer. Then she printed off a copy and went back to the reception area to hand it in to the desk clerk.

Sergeant McKenzie appeared a few minutes later, looking stern and businesslike, followed by Ross and Finn. The boy looked apprehensive, Katie thought, but Ross was doing his best to quietly reassure him. They spent some time talking to the sergeant about what was to happen in the next few days or weeks, but she didn't get to hear much of that conversation because Josh came over to her and took her to one side.

'It's good to see you again, Katie,' he said, laying his hand lightly on her elbow in a friendly gesture.

'You, too,' she murmured, smiling at him. Out of the corner of her eye she saw that Ross was looking their way. He was frowning, and she guessed he was put out by her apparent closeness with Josh. Of course, there was nothing at all between her and Josh except for friendship, but if Ross thought otherwise, so be it. She wasn't going to worry about that. Didn't he deserve to suffer a little after the way he'd behaved?

She tried to put him out of her mind for the moment and turned her attention back to Josh. 'I didn't realise you were going to be acting for Finn,' she said.

He nodded. 'I was given his case this morning. We seem to get on well together, and he wants me to go on working with him, so with any luck I'll be able to stay with the case through to the end. It all depends on the date for the court hearing, though, and who happens to be on duty at my firm that day. I could always try to change my schedule if I'm meant to be elsewhere.'

Katie was shocked. 'Will it come to that? I was hoping the sergeant would come to realise it was all a mistake.'

He grimaced. 'Unfortunately, Finn seems to have found himself mixed up with a gang of hooligans that has been causing mayhem in the area, and I think the sergeant has decided to come down hard on them. Anyway, it'll be up to the powers-that-be to decide whether any further action is to be taken. I'll write a report and send it off, and hope that it does some good.'

'Thanks, Josh.' She shook her head. 'I really can't see that Finn is guilty in all this. He's made mistakes in the past, but he's not a bad lad.'

He laid a reassuring hand on her shoulder. 'I'll do what I can for him, Katie.'

She nodded, but she was anxious, wishing that she could do something to put things right. Finn seemed so young, so out of his depth.

Ross came over to them. His blue eyes were cool as he noted the way Josh was standing, close to Katie, and Josh must have felt uncomfortable under that probing gaze because he coloured slightly and eased himself away from her a little.

'I saw you came here in a taxi,' Ross said, addressing Josh. 'Do you need a lift back? I'm going to take Finn home, but we can drop you off on the way if you like. Are you staying locally?'

'Thanks, Ross—yes, I'm renting the old corn mill. I'm afraid it's in the opposite direction from where Finn lives, though. I don't want to put you out. It's just that it's awkward for me at the moment because my car's at the garage—somebody backed into it on the ferry when I was coming over here.'

Katie quietly interrupted. 'My house is close to Finn's,' she said, glancing at Ross. 'My shift here's finished, so I could take the lad home. That will save you doubling back on yourself—it looks as though you and Josh are living fairly close to one another.'

Ross nodded. 'Okay. That sounds good.' He turned to Finn. 'Is that all right with you?'

'Yeah, that'll be fine.' Finn's face lit up. 'I can take Katie to see Baz.'

'Baz?' Katie frowned.

'He's Finn's latest good cause,' Ross supplied helpfully, his mouth making a wry shape. 'He came across an abandoned puppy this morning when he was helping the farmer cut down the overgrown hedge. At least, that's what we think happened to him. He was in a sorry state, huddled in the undergrowth, cold and shaking. I was working, so I couldn't deal with it right away, but it's a situation we need to sort out.' He frowned as he looked at Finn.

'He needs to go to the vet, Finn, and then maybe the RSPCA. I'm sorry, but I don't see any way you can keep him, and much as I'd like to take care of him, I can't have pets while I'm staying at McAskie's.'

'I'm not letting him go.' Finn's mouth set in a mutinous line. 'He came to me. He crawled over to me and put his paws on my legs. He wants me to help him. I know he's relying on me to look after him.'

'I do understand how you feel.' Ross put an arm around his brother. 'Like I said to you earlier, we'll talk it over and see if we can come to some agreement about what we're going to do.'

He gave Katie a thoughtful look a minute or two later, as he and Josh prepared to leave. It seemed as though he wanted to talk to her and attempt to clear the air between them, but that was never going to happen, given that they weren't alone, and Katie turned her head away. She was still smarting inside, upset and angry because he'd kept the news of his interview to himself all that time.

She went with Finn out to her car. 'So, is there something wrong with you having Baz at your house?' she asked, when he was settled in the passenger seat. 'What do your parents think about having him around? Aren't they very keen on the idea?'

He shook his head. 'Mum's okay with it, but Dad says it's too much work for her, even though I promised I would look after him. And, anyway, he doesn't want a dog around the place. He says he'll dig up the garden and chew the furniture to bits, and mess everywhere, but I said I wouldn't let him.'

'Well, actually, he has a point there, you know,' Katie said, as she started up the engine. She glanced at him. 'What are you going to do?'

'I don't know yet. But I'll think of something. If he gets this job he's after, maybe Ross will get a place of his own—he did talk about doing that—and then Baz could live there.'

Katie blinked. It hadn't occurred to her before this, but Finn was right. If Ross was successful in getting the job, it followed that he would need to live hereabouts. She was completely shaken by that thought. Ross, living here…

'I could stay with Ross, too. I know he would let me.' Finn pressed his lips together in the same way she'd seen Ross do many times, and her heart gave a small, unbidden lurch. She gave herself a mental shake. She had to get that man out of her mind. It was doing her no good at all to keep thinking of him this way.

She drove along the country lane towards the outskirts of the village. Finn lived in a small hamlet, in a house near a wooded area, and she had fond memories of the place. She had explored that woodland with her sister when they'd been teenagers, and often they had come across Ross and his friends there, too.

One day, she'd stretched out on the long, low branch of a tree and he'd come to stand beside her, talking to her about this and that. It had been an idyllic time, lying there in the warm sunshine, chatting, with Ross leaning negligently against the bole of the tree… Until Jessie had come along, that was. Jessie had been totally oblivious to the warm intimacy she was disturbing, and reluctantly Ross had straightened up and turned to greet her.

Katie determinedly pushed the image from her mind. 'Presumably your parents are looking after the puppy at the moment—until you can sort things out?'

Finn shook his head. 'My dad won't have him in the house. He told me to take him to the RSPCA, but I didn't. I couldn't. He's not very well, and I was afraid they might put him down. I couldn't let that happen,

Katie, so I put him in the shed. Dad never goes in there these days. I have to look after him. I've always wanted a dog, ever since I was little.'

Katie gave an inward sigh. The puppy was definitely going to be a problem, that was clear. 'What's wrong with him?' she asked. She guessed the puppy must be quite sick because Ross had said earlier that he needed to see a vet.

'He has a cough. And he shivers all the time and keeps retching, but I know he'll get better if I look after him. I can't let him go, Katie—he looks at me with his brown eyes as though he's pleading with me to take care of him. I can't let him down.'

Katie parked her car in the lane near the back of Finn's house. She turned to look at him. 'You know, Finn, I'm amazed that you care so much about this puppy, considering that you were bitten by a dog just a few days ago. Hasn't it put you off at all? They don't stay puppies for ever, you know.'

'No, it hasn't put me off.' He shook his head. 'Baz is really good-natured and he would never do anything like that. Besides, perhaps that other dog thought I was on its territory, and that's why he attacked me.' He frowned. 'He shouldn't have been there, though, out on the street. His owners should have kept him indoors or had him on a leash. That's what Sergeant McKenzie said, anyway. I think he's going to make them keep him in. I said I didn't want him to be put down, not if this was the first time he'd hurt anyone. I think he should have a second chance.'

'That's very generous of you, Finn.' She wasn't sure it was altogether a wise move, but no doubt Sergeant McKenzie would do the right thing.

They climbed out of the car and went through a gateway at the end of a long garden. Finn led the way along a short crazy-paving path. 'We have to be quiet,' he said, putting a finger to his lips. 'I don't want Mum and Dad to hear us.'

'All right.' She frowned. 'Do they know where you've been this evening?'

'No. They don't know anything about what's been happening. Ross said he'll have to tell them at some point, but he agreed to wait a while. He told Sergeant McKenzie he'd be responsible for me. If my dad knew what was going on I'd be grounded for weeks. He wouldn't believe I didn't do it.'

It was a sorry state of affairs, but Katie kept quiet and went with him to the shed. It was hidden by a trellis covered by an overgrown clematis. The windows were open, letting in warm air, and as they went in she could see that Finn had put down a dish of clean water for the puppy. Coming from the shadows, she heard hoarse, rasping sounds and a low, unhappy whining.

The puppy was huddled in a corner, lying on a couple of old towels. He was a boxer crossbreed, Katie guessed, about seven weeks old, a bundle of brown fur with a smudge of black around his nose, jaw and eyes, and there were white markings on his chest and paws. When he saw Finn, his tail began to thump happily, but it seemed he was too listless to get up and come to greet him.

'Hi, there, boy, how're you doing?' Finn crouched down beside him and lifted him carefully into his lap. 'Did you miss me? You don't look too good, young fella. Perhaps you should get some fresh air.'

Katie debated with herself what she should do. It was clear that the puppy meant a great deal to Finn, who obviously had a lot of pent-up love waiting to be poured out on to this vulnerable, abandoned creature.

'Wrap him up in the towel,' she told him, making up her mind, 'and we'll take him along to the vet. The surgery should still be open if we hurry.'

Finn's eyes widened. He didn't need to be urged on and, after taking the pup outside to let him relieve himself, he swiftly did as Katie suggested and hurried to her car, with Baz cradled to his chest.

His mobile phone rang as they drove to the next village and he reached into his jacket pocket to answer it.

'It's my brother,' he mouthed to her as he read the caller display. 'Hi, Ross. What's up?'

Katie couldn't hear what Ross was saying, but it became fairly clear from Finn's side of the conversation that Ross wanted to make arrangements for the puppy.

'We're headed to the vet's place now,' Finn told him. 'Katie said she'd deal with it. She said she'd pay the vet's bill—but I'm going to pay her back with the money I earn doing jobs on the farm.'

When the call ended, he turned to her. 'He said he'd already made an appointment for tomorrow morning, but he's going to cancel that now.'

Katie glanced at the puppy. 'We could have waited, I suppose, but he doesn't look very happy, does he? Poor little thing.'

A short time later, they arrived at the large house where the vet held his surgeries. It was a sprawling place, with several outbuildings that served as housing for the animals that needed to be watched overnight.

The vet was a big, kindly man in his fifties, with friendly eyes and dark hair that was beginning to show streaks of grey here and there. 'Who do we have here, then?' he asked, as Finn set his precious bundle down on the examination table.

'His name's Baz,' Finn told him. 'I found him hiding in some long grass near an old well. I think he must have been there all night. He came to me when I started to talk to him. He trusts me.'

The vet nodded. 'Let's have a look at him.' He looked fondly at the puppy and started to examine him carefully, beginning with his head, eyes and teeth, and then he checked each of his limbs in turn. He was listening to Baz's chest with his stethoscope when there was a knock at the door and Ross came into the surgery.

Katie stared at him. He must have set out for the surgery as soon as he'd finished talking to Finn. 'Sorry I'm late,' he said. 'How's he doing?'

The vet pushed his stethoscope back into his pocket. 'Hello, there, Ross.' He stroked the puppy's ears. 'It's kennel cough,' he answered, 'as I suspected when we talked on the phone this morning.'

Katie frowned. So Ross had already spoken to the vet?

'It's nothing too serious…a while back he probably inhaled some bacterial particles that have set up an irritation in his lungs. His immune system is probably weak, and that's made him vulnerable. A course of antibiotics should sort him out. In the meantime, he needs plenty of rest and a good diet, three to four meals a day for the next few weeks. And, of course, keep him away from other dogs until he's had all his vaccinations. We'll see to those once he's fit and healthy again.'

They left his office and trooped back to Reception, where Ross insisted on paying the bill instead of Katie. A few minutes later, when he was loaded up with medicines, puppy food and health supplements, they walked out to the car park and stood by the fence for a while, breathing in the fresh evening air. From here they looked out over meadowland, where sheep grazed against a backdrop of hills and valleys.

'I've been thinking about what's to be done with him, Finn,' Ross said. 'Are there any of your friends who could take him on?'

Finn shook his head. 'They all have dogs, or cats, already. I don't know what to do, Ross, except…you know you've always said you wanted a dog, and you'll be looking for a place of your own soon if you stay here, won't you? Can't I keep him in the shed for a while until we sort something out?'

'You know that won't work.' Ross's expression was rueful. 'It could be some time before I manage to buy a house over here. Several weeks at least.'

Katie's brows came together in a dark line. Was he so sure that he would get the job?

Ross pulled in a deep breath, and he must have known that his brother wouldn't like what he had to say. 'I could ask around and see if anyone will take him in. It's either that or the RSPCA, I'm afraid. Whatever happens, I'll make sure he'll be well looked after.'

Katie watched the puppy as he looked out at the world from Finn's arms. He was timid, unsure of himself at first, but soon his tail began to thump, and he started to pant in excitement. She smiled. He was adorable, a little lost soul who had no idea his fate was being mulled over this way.

'I suppose he could stay at my house for a while,' she heard herself say. The words were out of her mouth before she had time to think of the consequences. 'Jessie's staying there with me for a few weeks, and she'll be there sometimes during the day. Between us, we should be able to look after him.'

Her brows drew together. What had just happened? It wasn't at all like her to make snap decisions that would alter the tranquil, safe path of her life. Somehow, though, ever since Ross had turned up, her emotions and thought processes had been in chaos.

Perhaps something else was going on here, too. After seeing that tiny baby fighting for his life the other day at the hospital, her maternal instincts were all fired up. Much as she might have liked to have a family of her own, that wasn't on the cards right now, but for a short time, at any rate, maybe she could turn some of her instincts into caring for this sick little puppy.

She couldn't totally account for her impetuous action, but this was definitely something she wanted to do. 'But you will have to look after him most of all in the daytime, Finn,' she said, 'and you'll need to clean up after him and so on while we're out at work. Do you think you could do that?'

Finn's face lit up. 'Wow, yes. Thanks, Katie. That's a terrific idea. I'll come in between doing jobs on the farm.'

Ross's brows shot up as he looked from one to the other. 'Have you lost your senses?' he asked, sending a mystified look in her direction. 'Finn's a teenager, so I can understand how he might want to give in to his emotions this way, but you?' He shook his head. 'You're a grown woman, a doctor, with big responsibilities. Have you any idea what you're doing?'

Katie shrugged. 'I think so. I know it seems a wild thing to do but we always had dogs at home when I was growing up, and I think I've been missing that. The house seems empty somehow.'

'Hmm.' She guessed he still wasn't convinced. He was looking at her as though he feared she might be suffering from a fever of some sort. 'There is the problem of Finn finding work, of course,' he said. 'What's going to happen to the pup if he's not around to take care of him? Finn's not going back to school or college next term, so he's been thinking about what he's going to do. I'm not sure either of you are thinking this through. A dog needs exercise, fresh air and company.'

'I realise that but we'll cross that bridge when we come to it,' Katie said, standing her ground. 'If it comes to the worst, I'll perhaps ask Jack's mother if she would mind walking him for me. I think she would like to do that.' She was on friendly terms with her neighbour, and the little boy, Jack, was often at her house, playing in the garden or eating cookies in the kitchen.

Ross was shaking his head, and she braced her shoulders and faced up to him squarely. 'Either way, he's my problem now, so you don't have to give it any more thought.'

'If only it were that simple,' he said on a disbelieving note. 'My brother's landed us in this, and I feel duty bound to get involved, whether or not it's my responsibility.' He glanced at Finn. 'You'd better get him settled in the car. We need to find a late-opening pet store so that we can get him set up with all the equipment he needs.'

Finn nodded and hurried over to where the cars were parked. Katie had the feeling he wanted to escape before either of them decided to change the current plan of action.

She slanted Ross a quick look. 'It won't be necessary for you to shop around for stuff,' she said firmly. 'I'll see to all that. I'm sure you must have plenty of other things to do with your time. Like working out how Josh is going to keep Finn from going to court, for one thing, or planning out how you're going to run the A and E department if you get this new job, for another.'

His blue eyes shimmered as he scanned her slender form. 'Not at all, Katie. You can rest easy, that's all well in hand. You're my number-one priority right now, and if there's any way I can make life easier for you, I'll do it.'

'If that's true, perhaps you should have stayed on the mainland,' she said under her breath.

He laughed. 'Anything, excluding that,' he murmured. 'After all, I need to keep an eye on you, if only to make sure that Kilburn doesn't manage to weasel his way into your affections and turn your head.'

Her gaze was steady. 'Maybe he's already done that,' she said, in a flippant tone. It wouldn't do for Ross to harbour any ideas on that score—any more than he had already, at least. It was all a sham, but perhaps Josh was the one deterrent she could rely on.

Ross didn't answer, but his expression was brooding as he walked with her to her car, and she felt a tiny, inner smile of satisfaction begin to grow. It may not be much, but her rickety defence shield was settling into place.

CHAPTER SIX

'I'M SORRY, KATIE. I wanted you for this job, you know I did, but I was simply outvoted. You would have been an excellent choice, but some of the board members were set on having Ross McGregor. He's had experience in all sorts of hospitals all over the world, and it gave him the edge, but you mustn't be put off by any of that. You're a great doctor and you'll do well in your career. You just need to give it a little more time.'

Mr Haskins delivered the news gently, with a sympathetic smile, but he was only echoing what Katie had known inwardly from the moment she'd heard that Ross had applied for the post. It was galling to think that Ross was now her boss.

'Thanks for standing by me, anyway,' Katie murmured. Her disappointment was a dull, leaden feeling in her stomach. 'I suppose this means he'll be starting work straight away? Or does he have to give notice at his hospital on the mainland?'

He shook his head. 'They've agreed to let him start here right away, as they owe him quite a bit of time for holidays. I think it suits him to be over here just now, anyway.'

She nodded. That was true enough. Ross would be able to concentrate on dealing with Finn's troubles with the police, without having to worry about going back to his job over there. And, no doubt, he would already have started looking for a house.

Any thought that he would soon be leaving the island had melted away, and there would be no avoiding him now. She sighed inwardly. Her peace of mind had been well and truly shattered.

She struggled to drag her mind away from thoughts of Ross. Perhaps Finn's idea of going to live with his brother wasn't too far-fetched after all. Which meant her time with Baz would turn out to be far more short-lived than she had imagined. That, too, made her feel out of sorts. The vet had put up notices asking for information about anyone who might own the puppy, but as there had been no takers, Finn could now lay claim to him.

Baz had settled in really well at the house, and he'd even grown considerably in the last couple of weeks. He was healthier now, after all the romps in the garden in the sunshine and fresh air, and the cough and the listlessness were virtually a thing of the past. She found herself looking forward to seeing him at the end of the day.

'I should get back to work.' She excused herself from her boss's office and headed back to the triage area.

'Would you take a look at the baby in room one first of all?' Shona asked as Katie went over to the desk and glanced at the white board. 'She's six months old, having trouble with her breathing, and has a low-grade fever. I've put her on oxygen, but she's struggling, poor little thing.'

Katie nodded. 'Okay, I'll do that right away.' She glanced at the white board once more, and frowned. 'It says there that Ross McGregor is overseeing her case— perhaps I would do better looking at other patients?'

Shona shook her head. 'He's overseeing all the cases. I think he has it in mind to change the way we do things here. Nothing's actually been said to that effect, but you know how it is, you get the feeling that's going to happen.'

'Yes, I know what you mean.' He wasn't one to let the grass grow under his feet, was he?

Katie went in search of the baby, and found her sitting on her mother's lap, crying fretfully.

Shona had already linked her to the monitors, so that Katie could see straight away that the infant's blood oxygen level was low and her heart rate was well above normal.

Katie introduced herself to the mother, and after talking to her for a minute or two about the baby's condition she began to examine the infant. 'She'll be fine staying where she is, in your arms,' she murmured. 'I just need to listen to her chest, and I'll check her ears and throat.'

'She's not been taking her bottle properly these last few days,' her mother said. 'She can't breathe properly while she's feeding and she brings it back up again.'

'Yes, unfortunately that often happens with this kind of illness.' Katie folded away her stethoscope and pushed it down into her jacket pocket. 'She's having quite a bit of trouble with her chest and her blood oxygen level is quite low, so I think we need to admit her for a few days. We'll keep her on humidified oxygen, and I'll prescribe medication to ease the problems in her lungs.' She glanced at the woman, a pretty, dark-haired girl in her twenties. 'Do you have any questions you'd like to ask me?'

'Not really—only that I want to stay with her. Will that be okay?'

Katie nodded, and said with a smile, 'Of course. I'll ask the nurse to come and talk to you about that.'

'Thanks.'

The mother adjusted the baby's clothing, and then cradled her child over her shoulder to try to ease the congestion in her chest. Katie watched them, her mouth curving softly. That maternal tug at her heart was back again in full force, and she realised she was reluctant to move away to go and write up the infant's chart.

'Is everything in hand here?' Ross came into the room a minute or so later, as she finished talking to the nurse who was assisting. Katie stiffened, immediately on edge, but if Ross noticed, he gave no sign of it. He nodded to the mother and then spoke to Katie in a low voice. 'How is it going? Are you admitting the baby?'

'Yes. I've ordered tests, but I suspect it's bronchiolitis on top of a viral infection.' She finished writing up the chart and then looked at him as they walked together to the triage area.

Today he was wearing a dark, beautifully tailored suit, with the jacket undone to reveal a crisp, pale-coloured shirt teamed with a subtly patterned tie. He looked good, as ever, and she wished he didn't always have this effect on her of making her heart beat that little bit faster and bringing warm colour to her cheeks. She tucked a strand of burnished chestnut hair behind her ear and pulled in a deep breath.

'I know you've been to see Mr Haskins,' he said, throwing her a quick, cautious look, 'so you must have heard the news about the job.'

She nodded. 'Were you expecting me to congratulate you?' That sounded churlish, she knew, and she regretted the words as soon as they were out. She clamped her mouth shut.

He shook his head and said quietly, 'I'm sorry it had to come at your expense.' He sent her an oblique glance. 'Do you think you'll be able to come to terms with it?'

Her expression was grim. 'That might take a while.' She didn't want to talk about the effect his promotion had had on her. Instead, she said tautly, 'It'll mean a big change for you, won't it? After all, you're not used to staying in one place long, are you? Finn said you'd never put down roots anywhere before this. Does that mean you're planning on using this as a stop-gap? Perhaps you'll be moving on again in a couple of years or so.'

For her, it would have been the culmination of a long-term ambition, an opportunity to establish herself here, close to the place where she had lived her whole life. She had envisaged the changes she might make, and she knew deep down that she would have stayed here for years to come, doing the job she loved.

'There's always that possibility, I suppose, but I must say this job is pretty much everything I've been aiming for. I'll be in overall control of the A and E departments here—adult and paediatric—and I'll have a say in the administration of the wider region.' He made a wry smile. 'I expect that will keep me occupied for quite some time.'

'So you'll be buying a house over here? That must be another new experience for you.' The fact of him being here was something she had to get used to, but as yet she had no idea how she would deal with it.

They reached the main desk, and Katie studied the board for the name of her next patient.

'It is.' He nodded. 'I'm looking forward to it. Actually, I've already put in an offer for the Loch Sheirach property. Do you remember how we used to go over there and look at it when we were in our teens? It's been empty for a few weeks so, if the owner accepts, things could start to move quickly.'

Her heart gave an uncomfortable lurch. He was buying that house, out of all others? What more could he do to turn the knife?

'I do. It's a lovely house,' she said on a wistful note. She passed by the loch occasionally, whenever she took the scenic route home, and she always looked for a glimpse of the white-painted house that nestled in the wooded valley.

It was the sort of house she dreamed about, with two large gables, several chimneys and an extended south side. There were plenty of large windows from which she guessed there would be magnificent views over the loch.

'I've always thought so,' he agreed. 'I'm lucky that it's come on sale just at the right time for me.'

'Who'd have thought you would ever come back to the island to stay?' she murmured distractedly. 'When you left, all those years ago, you hinted that you might not return. There was a lot of bad feeling at the time and no one would ever have imagined you would be keen to settle down here, ever again.'

His mouth slanted. 'I was very young. I've had plenty of time since then to work through my resentment and disillusion, and I've learned to put it to one side. Besides, there are other reasons for me to want to be back here.' He was silent for a moment, his blue eyes brooding as he met her gaze, and for a second or two a flicker of deep-seated emotion burned in her heart. Was he hinting that he wanted to be with her?

She quickly quelled that thought. They might have got close once or twice in the past, and recently there was no denying that an attraction existed between them, but she wasn't naive enough to believe that Ross was suddenly ready to settle down into a relationship.

'Other reasons?' she queried, keeping a level tone.

He straightened, frowning, and she had a horrible feeling that he'd read her mind.

'Yes,' he said quietly. He hesitated. 'Finn, for instance. He's at a difficult age and he needs guidance, someone who will listen to him and understand his point of view.'

She swallowed hard, struggling to bring her conflicting emotions under control. What had she expected? Did she really think he might want to be here just for her? She said softly, 'And your father isn't the one to do that, or his mother?'

He shook his head. 'My father is very single-minded, and doesn't often take note of any point of view if it differs from his own. As to Finn's mother, she loves him dearly, but she won't go against my father.'

'That's unfortunate.' She sent him an oblique glance. 'You're obviously still not thinking about trying for a reconciliation?'

He gave a short, resigned laugh. 'I've spoken to my father since I've been back here, believe me, I've tried, but he's a hard man to deal with. He bottles things up inside, and whatever's gone on in the past, he's not prepared to forgive and forget. He didn't like the fact that I left, or that I joined the army.' He hesitated and a bleak look of resignation flickered in his dark eyes. 'There doesn't seem to be any moving on where he's concerned.'

Something in his expression tugged at her emotions and a sudden rush of sympathy overrode any self-imposed warnings about not getting involved with him. Beneath his rugged, self-contained exterior she caught a glimpse of the confused young boy who was struggling to understand what lay behind the actions of his remote and unyielding father.

'It must be really difficult for you.' She felt an overwhelming urge to put her arms around him and show him that she cared, but that would have been foolhardy in the extreme, so instead she sucked in a quick breath and said cautiously, 'Have you any idea why you and he find it so difficult to get along? After all, you're his son, his firstborn. He must surely care for you, deep down. Perhaps he doesn't know how to show it?'

He frowned. 'You may be right. I don't know why we couldn't sort things out. As you know, I reacted badly after my mother died, but that wasn't all of it. Perhaps I blamed him for being away on business all the time. Who knows? Maybe he felt guilty about that, too, but he couldn't show it. He always hid his feelings behind a tough exterior.'

He sighed. 'Whatever the reason, we never hit it off. We were never really close. And I was the sort of boy who was into everything, exploring, climbing and getting into trouble. The total opposite of him, in fact.'

'Yes. He strikes me as being a serious man, a businessman through and through.' She picked up a patient's file. 'Perhaps he thought you should be at home, studying, the way he used to. He put a lot of store by qualifications, didn't he?'

'You're probably right. It used to irritate him that I'd sneak out of the house when I should have been working on a project of some sort.'

She smiled inwardly. The fact was, Ross was a natural when it came to his studies. He didn't need to work at it. The knowledge was always there, at his fingertips. It came easily to him.

'I think at first I was relieved that he was away so much,' he said, 'but after a while I started to question it. He often left me to be looked after by relatives while he was out of town, and then one day he introduced me to the woman who was to become my stepmother, and I was shocked, through and through. I couldn't accept her. As a child, I felt they were being disrespectful to my mother's memory.'

'I'm so sorry,' she said softly. She ran her hand lightly over his arm in an intimate, warm gesture, and immediately he moved closer to her, his hand coming to rest on the small of her back. She faltered, realising how she had inadvertently let her guard down. 'But you get on well enough with Stephanie nowadays, don't you?'

'I do.' He smiled. 'She was very patient with me.'

'That's good.' Her gaze was thoughtful, pondering. 'Perhaps she might act as the bridge between you and your father so that you could come to an understanding?'

He chuckled. 'You never give up, do you?' he said, giving her a quick squeeze and sending her an amused glance. 'I think that must be one of the reasons I'm so fond of you, Katie—you're very straightforward, you never give up on something you believe in and you seem to have a deep-seated need for people to get along with one another.'

He studied her contemplatively, his eyes smokily blue. 'What a pity you can't take things that one stage further where you and I are concerned. We would do so well together.'

His expression was so intense the breath caught in her throat and she averted her gaze so that she wouldn't see the fierce glitter of his eyes. It was too unsettling and made her think about what she wanted deep down, of her heart's desire, and that was completely out of the question. He might promise her the earth, but who could tell how soon it would be before he moved on to some other fancy?

'I'm afraid that's not going to happen,' she said flatly. 'I've learned from my mistakes, and one thing I've realised is that I need a man with commitment and staying power, among other things, and that's not what you're about, is it? From what I've heard, you've never had the slightest urge to settle down with one woman for any length of time.'

She thought about that for a moment or two. Hadn't he admitted that he was afraid of being hurt? If he were to give his heart and soul to a woman, only to have her reject him, wouldn't the pain be as great for him as it had been when he'd lost his mother?

But there were other forces at work here, too, she suspected. 'Perhaps somewhere along the line, by taking up with Stephanie in what you thought was too soon after your loss, your father's given you the wrong idea about relationships.'

'You could be right about that,' he murmured. 'I've no doubt my father has a lot to answer for. But it doesn't have to mean that you and I can't have some fun, does it? You've always been very special to me, Katie.'

She lifted a brow. 'As the one that got away?'

'You're such a cynic. As the woman I'd most like to date,' he countered. His smile was rueful.

She wished that could be so but wasn't the truth that Ross liked to keep his options open?

'I think you're forgetting you're my boss now,' she said. 'And it wouldn't be at all professional for you and I to get involved, would it? Even if I was inclined to entertain the idea,' she hastened to add.

'I mean, people would talk, and I'm pretty sure that sooner or later they'd probably start to complain that we're in cahoots over any new strategies you decide to introduce. Or, heaven forbid, they might think you're favouring me in some way. You know how things work in hospitals once the grapevine gets going—all sorts of rumours and speculations get bandied about.'

He bent his head towards her. 'I've never paid much heed to what people think I should, or shouldn't, do. And as to favours...' he chuckled '...I don't need much incentive where you're concerned.' His warm glance drifted over her.

Her cheeks flooded with hot colour and she moved away from him. 'I'm serious about this,' she said in exasperation. 'I can't think why I'm wasting my time standing here, talking to you. I've patients to see. Perhaps you should go and check on some of the other children going through triage? There might be a really important case you need to deal with.'

'You're right,' he murmured, giving her one last, appraising glance before he switched his attention to the list of patients on the white board. 'And I'm headed for the assessment rooms right now. I'm sure some of these small patients would be better treated by nurses rather than doctors—that's the first of the strategies I'm about to introduce. It would free up the doctors' time and allow them to concentrate on the more serious cases. Excuse me...'

Too late, she realised that she was standing in his way, but with a smile he brushed past her, leaving her in a state of utter confusion. Their bodies had touched for a fleeting moment, his hands resting for a fraction of a second on her hips as he'd sought to steady her, and yet that searing contact had had quite the opposite effect. Her limbs had turned to jelly and she was left to stare after him and wonder how it was he managed to do that to her.

It was only as she walked over to the treatment bay to see her next patient that she realised he had been talking about starting up a nurse-led unit. His first day here and he was already working out ways that would disrupt her carefully organised system. She pressed her lips together. It just wasn't going to work, was it, the two of them working in the same unit?

She was still smarting over the changes he had in mind when she drove home at the end of her shift. The sky was overcast, dark, and threatening rain. It seemed to match her mood perfectly.

The minor injuries unit was only the first of several plans, she'd learned that day, and it seemed as though everything she'd set up was about to be thrown into disarray. 'Don't take it to heart,' Ross had said when she'd tackled him about it. 'It doesn't mean that your practices are being abandoned—I'm making small adjustments here and there, that's all. It'll all work more smoothly in the end, you'll see.'

'Will it?' Sparks had flown as she'd turned her gaze on him. 'So taking my nurses away is going to make life easier, is it? For whom? You should try working in A and E when members of staff are off sick, or on holiday, and you have to rely on agency nurses to fill the gaps. Do you know anything at all about the shortage of nurses these days?'

He was completely unruffled by her outburst. 'There's the thing, you see, people don't like change, especially when they're comfortable with what they've been doing for years on end—but once you get used to it, you'll see the advantages.'

'Or so you hope. There's something to be said for altering the status quo, but you don't have to throw out everything. Just because it's the tradition to do things a certain way it doesn't mean it's all bad.'

'I agree with you, and that's why I think we should work together on this,' he said thoughtfully. 'I respect the fact that you were a strong contender for this job, and I'm sure we'll make a good team. I'm relying on you to let me know when you think I'm taking a step too far. In this case, though, I've a clear idea what I want to do.'

Obviously her words had no effect on him whatsoever. He was determined to go ahead with his plans. She had been so annoyed that she'd turned away from him and had gone to find her next patient before she'd completely lost her cool.

She hadn't seen him again before she'd set off for home, and perhaps that was just as well. He was the boss now, and it wouldn't do for them to be airing their differences in front of the rest of the department.

Jessie was still at work when Katie walked into the farmhouse kitchen and set her bag down on the table. She carefully laid her jacket over the back of a chair and glanced towards the corner of the room where Baz had his bed. He had been curled up in there, fast asleep, but now he jumped up to greet her, his tail thumping madly.

'Have you missed me?' she said, gently tickling his ears. 'I wonder what you've been up to today?' She looked around and saw the remains of what had originally been a rubber dumbbell scattered on the tiled floor. 'I think I can guess. What's this, has Finn been buying you some new toys?'

He trotted away to fetch his favourite ball from his

box in the corner of the room, and came back to circle round and round against her legs, eager for her to stroke him, his tail going ten to the dozen.

'All right,' she said. 'We'll go into the garden and I'll throw your ball for you. But not for too long, I'm afraid, because I have to put the supper on and, besides, it looks as though it's about to rain.'

She looked at him, a brown and white bundle of energy, so different from the waif and stray he'd been just a short time ago. Somehow he managed to lift her spirits in a flash. What did he care about hospital budgets and patients' waiting times and targets and so on? Lots of playtime and plenty of food were the only things on his agenda, apart from cuddles from all and sundry. Life was bliss, as far as he was concerned.

It started to rain later as she was chopping up onions for the casserole she was making, and she glanced up at the ceiling, where a dark patch had begun to form because of water that had been seeping into the plaster over the past few months. There was still no sign of a workman who would come and fix the leak in the roof. This part of the house was a single-storey extension, and she guessed some of the roof tiles needed to be replaced.

'They're all too busy,' Jessie said, interpreting her glance as she came into the room and shook the raindrops from her coat. 'I've rung them several times, but I think the job's too small for them—we keep getting pushed to the back of the queue.'

'I guessed as much.' Katie finished putting together the casserole ingredients and slid the dish into the oven. 'How was your day?'

Her sister sat down on the floor, next to Baz, teaching him to sit and stay and offering him a treat whenever he did the right thing. 'It was okay. Dad's thinking of making use of some overgrown areas of the estate, and I've been helping him with the plans, in between stints in the gift shop.' She looked at Baz. 'Do you know, he's so clever, he's very easy to train.'

Katie smiled. 'That's because he gets to eat loads of goodies in the process. But you're right. He's house-trained already. We haven't had one accidental puddle in the last couple of days.'

They talked for a while, and then she started on her chores while the casserole cooked in the oven, working her way through a stack of ironing, while Jessie ran the vacuum cleaner over the carpets upstairs.

The doorbell rang as she was getting the puppy's supper ready, and he looked at her anxiously as she left his bowl on the worktop and went to see who was there. 'It's all right, I've not forgotten about you,' she told him, but a frown creased his soft brow as he saw the prospect of dinner fading away before his eyes.

'Forgotten about me? I should hope not,' Ross said, as she opened the door. 'I know it's been a few hours since we were last together, but even so.'

'Oh,' she murmured, her eyes widening. 'I wasn't expecting you.' She stared at him in shock, wondering what he was doing there. Realising how ungracious she sounded, she said quickly, 'I was talking to the dog. I mean…hello. What are you doing here?' Then, before he could answer, she pulled herself together and started again. 'Would you like to come in?'

'If that's okay with you?' He gave her a quizzical look. 'You're still speaking to me, then?'

She frowned. Sooner or later they had to find a way to get along with one another. 'I wasn't in the best of moods earlier, was I? It all came as a bit of a shock, what you were saying, I'll admit.' She shrugged. 'But

I've talked it through with Baz since then, and he seems to think, what the heck, as long as we get three square meals a day—or four, in his case—it'll all come right in the wash.'

He laughed. 'It sounds as though you and he are getting along just fine.' He walked with her to the kitchen. 'Actually, he's the reason I'm here. I've brought some more food for him. It's in the boot of the car—a big bag of puppy meal and some tins of meat. Is he allowed meat yet?'

'If he had his way, he'd eat whatever's going.' She gave a wry smile. 'But, yes, we've been giving him small amounts. I guess he likes it, because he always licks the bowl clean.'

The puppy gave a mournful gulp and she quickly put him out of his misery and gave him his supper. 'You didn't have to buy his food, you know,' she told Ross. 'I said I'd see to everything.'

'I know you did, but I think it's only right if I pay. We've imposed on you enough as it is.'

'I'm glad to do it. My only worry is that I won't want to hand him back when the time comes.' She waved him to a chair by the table. 'Sit down and I'll make us a drink. Would you like tea, or coffee?'

'Tea would be great, thanks.' He sat down and looked around the kitchen, admiring the décor, while Katie checked the casserole in the oven. It was almost ready.

'I'm about to serve up dinner,' she said, wondering if she ought to invite him to stay. Jessie would be aghast if she let him go without doing the neighbourly thing. As long as she kept him at arm's length, it wouldn't matter, would it? 'It'll easily stretch. Would you like to stay and eat with us?'

'Ah, I couldn't help noticing that wonderful smell.'

His brow furrowed. 'I don't want to impose on you, though. I only came to see how things were with you, and how Baz was doing...and to bring the food, of course.'

'You're very welcome to stay.'

'Then thank you. I'd like that.'

She gave another wry smile. 'Anyway, Jessie will be glad to see you.'

'She's here? I didn't realise that.' He tickled the puppy as he came over to him for some fuss, stroking his head and running his fingers over Baz's chest when he rolled over on his back in a submissive pose.

'She's busy upstairs at the moment, but I expect she'll be down in a while. I'll start to serve up the food.'

'Can I do anything to help? I could lay the table if you like.'

'Thanks. Cutlery's in the drawer over there.'

He washed his hands at the sink and then looked around admiringly. 'Have you done up the kitchen yourself, or was it already like this when you moved in?' he asked as he started to set out knives and forks. 'It looks really good. Very homely. I like the colour scheme and the glass-fronted cupboards. And the oak shelving is a lovely contrast.'

'I'm glad you like it. I did it when I first moved in here. I wasn't sure before I started if I was doing the right thing, choosing a colour that was a mixture between pale blue and green, but I think it turned out all right in the end.'

He nodded. 'It looks great.'

'Hmm.' Her expression was rueful. 'Except for the damp patch on the ceiling. There's a leak somewhere, either from the tiles or in the roofing felt or both. I just can't get a workman to come out and fix it.'

He studied the area she pointed out. 'After we've eaten, I'll have a look in the attic for you to see if I can find out where the problem is.'

'Oh, but you don't have to do that, really. I'm sure I'll be able to sort something out, it's just that it's taking a while. We'll be okay as long as the plaster holds.'

'It's no problem,' he said with a smile. 'Besides, if you're going to feed me, it's the least I can do, especially since I seemed to upset you earlier today. I didn't mean to do that, you know. I just have so many ideas about how to run things, and I may tend to get carried away with them sometimes. It's just as well that you're able to point out some of the pitfalls to me, like the nursing situation, for example. We'll have to find ways of getting around the problem.'

His expression sobered. 'Are you very disappointed about not getting the job? Will it make you think about moving on and applying somewhere else? I'd hate that to happen.'

'I was upset, of course.' She gave a light shrug. 'Until you came along, I was foremost in the running to get it. It's what I've worked for and I would have enjoyed the challenge and the responsibility. But once I knew you had applied for the post, I was pretty sure you would be taking over.' She took warm plates from the grill and set them out on the table.

Jessie came into the room and exclaimed with delight when she saw Ross. 'Hi, there,' she said, giving him a beautiful smile. 'I'm so glad you dropped by. Katie told me that you got the job she was after—is that going to cause trouble for you two?'

'I hope not.'

'Possibly. Who can tell?'

Ross and Katie both answered at once, and Ross gave

a wry smile. 'We'll have to find a way to sort things out between us,' he said.

'Hmm. If it doesn't work out for you, I'm always here to lend an ear. I'm a good listener.' Jessie was in a teasing mood, and Katie left her to chat to Ross while she fetched the casserole from the oven.

'This is delicious,' Ross said a short time later as he tucked into braised beef and tender vegetables. 'They serve up good meals at McAskie's but nothing to compare with this. I can't remember the last time I had a home-cooked meal. It's the one thing I really miss.'

Katie was startled. 'Do you never cook for yourself—surely you must have done from time to time?'

'Sometimes,' he admitted, 'but only basic stuff. Anything you can have on toast, or maybe a grilled steak, or pizza, but beyond that I'm hopeless.'

'Oh, I don't know about that,' Jessie put in, smiling. 'I remember a long time ago when you bought a throw-away barbecue pack and cooked sausages for us down by the river. I thought it was the best meal I'd ever tasted.'

'Well, you were younger then.' He laughed. 'I don't suppose you even cared about the blackened bits. They probably just added to the adventure.'

They reminisced over old times for a while, ending the meal with a fresh fruit salad, and then Katie made coffee while Jessie and Ross stacked the crockery in the dishwasher.

'Why don't you let me show you around the place?' Jessie said, when they were finished. She tucked her arm into Ross's and urged him towards the sitting room.

Ross turned as they headed out of the kitchen. 'I've not forgotten about the leak, Katie,' he said. 'I'll take a look at it as soon as we're done.'

Katie nodded, and absently stroked the puppy's fur as he came to her. 'I guess it's just you and me, then, Baz,' she murmured into the emptiness of the kitchen. It was strange how painfully it wrung her heart to have Ross here in her home. Every instinct told her that falling for him would be a big mistake. He was her boss, and that was a definite no-no.

The situation was fraught with danger. She fought against her feelings for him at every turn, yet she was fast coming to the conclusion that it was a losing battle, and that scared her.

She'd been hurt once before, but deep down she knew this time would be different. This time there would be no recovering from a broken heart.

CHAPTER SEVEN

JOSH MOVED THE large terracotta container to a sunny spot on the patio and glanced up at Katie. 'Is it okay for you if I put it here?'

'That's just fine. Thanks, Josh.' The hybrid rose looked good in its new position, and the delicate fragrance drifted on the air to where Katie stood by the open patio doors. She smiled. 'I can see I shall have to start building up some muscles if I'm going to get into gardening in a big way.'

He gave a mock grimace. 'Please don't do that. Anything you want done, you know you only have to ask.'

'Thanks. I appreciate that. Usually, Jessie and I manage things between us, but that container is particularly heavy.'

He nodded. 'I wondered if Jessie might be with you today. She doesn't work every weekend on the family estate, does she?'

'No, she doesn't, but she had to go over to her house to see how the extension's coming along, and then she said she was going shopping. She's in desperate need of some new clothes, apparently.'

Jessie had confided that she wanted to find a new outfit for the barbecue being held at McAskie's Bar the next weekend. 'Ross will be there,' she'd said. 'It'll be great fun. I'm really looking forward to it.'

'I expect it will be a great day.' Katie had glanced at her sister. 'You like him, don't you?"

Jessie had nodded. 'He's a good person,' she'd said, her voice quiet and distant as though she had been preoccupied in some way. 'He's not at all bad, the way some people think of him, like Mum and Dad, for instance.' She'd sighed. 'I owe him so much.'

'What do you mean?' Katie had asked, but Jessie had simply shrugged.

'Nothing. Nothing at all. Take no notice of me. I guess I'm rambling a bit.'

Katie had frowned. Something had obviously been on Jessie's mind and had been, in fact, since Ross had returned from the mainland. She'd often been distant lately, lost in thought.

'Are you all right?' Josh's voice brought her back to the present. 'You suddenly have a far-away look in your eyes.'

'Do I? Sorry.' Hastily, she made an effort to pull herself together. 'Yes, I'm fine.' She bent down to inspect the gnarled stick that Baz dropped at her feet. 'That's great, Baz,' she murmured. 'But enough of throwing sticks for now. Go and find your hide chew bone. It's around here somewhere.' She straightened up and looked at Josh once more. 'I suppose I was wondering if she's going to break the bank with her purchases.'

He laughed. 'That's a strong possibility, I guess. She always looks good, doesn't she?' He glanced around. 'Is there anything else you need moved before I go? I have to drop by the office to see to some urgent paperwork, otherwise I'd be tempted to stay longer. It's so peaceful here—so different from the frantic world I live in day to day.'

'Yes, it is. I find I need to come out here after a busy day in Emergency. It helps to calm me down.' She looked around the garden, at the bird table where colourful finches came to see what titbits were on offer, and the shrubbery where bright yellow gorse and deep blue wallflowers vied for space.

'There's nothing else that needs doing, thanks. You've been a great help. And it was good of you to come over and let me know about Finn's case. I've been worrying about him.'

'I know. We've both known him all his life and it's bound to be upsetting to see him getting into trouble. Ross has been into the office regularly to make sure that everything that can be done is being done—but we've finally sent off our statements, disputing the so-called evidence, so all we can do now is wait.

'And as for Finn's injury—the dog owner has been reprimanded and has to obey strict conditions, otherwise the dog will be taken from him. He's very lucky that he was given a reprieve. I think Finn had a lot to do with that.'

'By all accounts the owner was pretty shaken up by the whole thing, almost as much as Finn. He apologised and told Finn the dog was spooked by something and ran out of the house when the door was opened. He must have thought Finn was on his territory.'

Josh nodded. 'Finn's lucky the outcome wasn't much worse.' They walked along the path to the front of the house, and there Josh turned to give her a hug and a quick kiss on the cheek. 'Don't forget, any time you need me to help you with anything, you only have to call.'

'I won't. Thanks, Josh.'

He hugged her again and then reluctantly walked to his car. Glancing across the drive, it was only then that Katie noticed another vehicle was parked at the roadside. Ross's car.

Ross nodded briefly to Josh and then came along the path towards her, his eyes narrowed. Even as she waved goodbye to Josh she felt the intensity of Ross's gaze fixed on her.

'You and Josh seem to be getting along very well,' he said on a thoughtful note. 'Like a house on fire, I'd say.'

She nodded. 'We always did. Is that a problem for you?'

'Not at all,' he murmured. He glanced back at Josh's car, now fast disappearing along the road. 'At least, it's nothing a well-aimed garden hose wouldn't put right.'

She laughed. 'You're a wicked man, Ross McGregor. Always have been...'

'Hmm, I deny it all. I'm the very soul of innocence. I believe in looking after my own, that's all.'

She gave him a chiding look. 'That's very presumptuous of you, don't you think?'

'Not at all.' He slid his arms around her waist. 'You're definitely mine, always have been. You just don't know it yet. You look gorgeous, by the way.' He moved in closer.

'I hardly think so, but thanks all the same.' It was good that he thought so, and his comment made her feel warm inside. She was dressed for gardening, in jeans that moulded themselves to her figure, along with a loose-fitting shirt, and she'd pinned her hair back so that her curls were held away from her cheeks.

Smiling, she evaded his seeking mouth as he bent to kiss her, and she managed to wriggle out of his grasp, gently pushing him away.

'Behave yourself, Ross. It won't do at all. I work for you now, remember? Tell me why you're here.' Her expression changed. 'Is it a problem with Finn?'

'No, nothing like that.' He accepted defeat with good grace. 'The opposite, in fact.' He shook his head. 'Finn's doing all right. He had the stitches removed from his wound, and everything's healing up nicely. You did a great job there with the sutures. With any luck there'll only be the faintest of scars.'

'I'm glad about that. How's he doing otherwise? I don't often get to see him now—I gave him a key to the house so he can come to see Baz, but then he goes off to work on the farm before I get home.'

'He's bearing up well, and he's been full of enthusiasm ever since you had a word with your father and arranged for him to have a job on the estate.' He studied her, his gaze intent and appreciative. 'I didn't realise you were going to talk to your father about him. That was very thoughtful of you. I appreciate it, and so does Finn.'

He slid his arm around her as they walked round the house towards the garden, and she tried not to let the closeness affect her. He was clearly not taking any notice of her protests.

'I talked things over with Finn,' she said. 'I know he has always loved being outdoors, and working in forestry is something that will suit him perfectly, I think.'

'It will. He's even talking about doing a college course.'

'Yes, my father will arrange all that for him. He looks after his workers. He likes to see them get their qualifications and do well.'

He nodded. 'Yes, well, by way of returning the favour ever so slightly, I'm here to fix the tiles on your roof.

I've managed to find matching ones, and once they're in place they should put a stop to your problems.'

A rush of anxiety overwhelmed her all of a sudden and she said hurriedly, 'You don't have to do that, Ross. In fact, I'd really rather you didn't. You're not a roofer—what if you slipped and fell? I couldn't bear to have that on my conscience.' She didn't want him up there, trying to keep his balance while he removed broken tiles and fixed new ones in place.

'Thanks for your concern,' he said softly, 'but there's no need for you to worry. I'll be fine. It's something I need to do.' They came to the garden, and he gazed around, smiling at the pleasing picture it made, with the carefully planted rockery and the green expanse of lawn that was edged on one side with a wide border filled with cottage-garden flowers. 'You've worked hard on this the last few weeks. It looks a picture.'

'Thanks. I was determined to get to grips with it.'

'Maybe you could help me to plan out my garden at Loch Sheirach? It's been left to grow a little wild, but there are some elements I'd like to keep.'

Her eyes widened. 'You managed to buy the property, then? It's yours?'

'It is. The paperwork and tying up all the loose ends will take some time, but I've signed the contract. I'd really like your input on how I should do the place up. You've an eye for making a house look homely and welcoming.'

She swallowed her dismay at him owning the house she loved. 'I'll be glad to help.' At least she would get to see the place and have a small part in its renovation. She smiled at him, despite her feelings, pleased that things were working out for him. He returned her gaze until they gradually became aware that the garden wasn't quite so tranquil any more.

Baz was hunting among the flowers, his nose burrowing into the wood chippings that Katie had spread between the plants, and bits were flying in all directions as he nudged them out of the way.

'Baz, stop that right now,' she said, worried about the precious blooms that were being flattened. The scent of crushed lavender wafted on the air as he trampled the nearby shrub.

In response to her sharp admonition, he looked up at her briefly, wagging his tail, and then his nose dipped down again into the earth. A moment later he padded over to her, triumphantly holding his chew bone between his teeth. Pleased with himself, he dropped it at her feet.

'Well, yes, thank you. You are a clever little man, I must say, and I did ask you to go and find it, but you have to leave my flowers alone, do you hear?'

Ross chuckled as Baz came to him for some attention. He stroked him and patted his flanks. 'He's certainly made himself at home here, hasn't he? Are things working out all right with Finn coming to walk him every day?'

She nodded. 'Finn's been great with him. He's taught him to sit and stay and to fetch things. He has a great nose on him—Baz, I mean, not Finn. He's always hunting things out.' She frowned. 'I shall miss him when he goes but from the sound of things, it won't be too long before that happens, will it? Finn says he's planning on moving in with you. I'm not sure that's a good thing. He's very young to be leaving home.'

'It was his idea, and I've told him it's okay with me as long as he squares it with my father and Stephanie first. I don't think they'll be too pleased, and I'd prefer it if he stayed on good terms with both of them.' He pressed his lips together briefly. 'Things haven't been going too well for him at home, though. I had to tell my father about the bail situation and he's very annoyed. I put it to him the best way I could, but he went off like a rocket all the same.'

They went over to the chairs that were set out on the patio and sat down by the wrought-iron table. 'As for the dog, it'll be a couple of weeks before I move into the house, and then when I'm settled, after, say, another week, Baz can come to stay with me. My only problem is what I'm going to do to make sure he's looked after in the daytime while Finn and I are both at work. It was never a good idea to take him on.'

She nodded. 'I know. I've been thinking about that, too.' Her green eyes were troubled. She really would miss the puppy when he left her.

'I'll do my best to find a reliable dog walker.' He studied her, taking in the unhappy jut of her mouth. 'It'll make life easier for you, Katie, and you know you can come and see us any time. You could even stay over, if you wanted, for as long as you liked. Purely for Baz, of course.' There was a wicked gleam in his eyes that belied his innocence, and Katie smiled wryly.

'That would be great,' she said, with a spark of mischievousness in her glance. 'I know Baz would absolutely love to have me stay with him.'

She poured juice from a jug on the table and handed him a glass. 'Gardening's thirsty work,' she murmured, topping up her own glass, 'especially in this sunshine. I've been deadheading and generally tidying up for the last couple of hours.'

'Was that why Josh was here, to help out?' He accepted the drink she offered him and took a long swallow, watching her over the rim.

She smiled. 'No, although he did help with some heavy lifting. He came to tell me how things were going with Finn, and what was happening with the case. I think it will take a while longer before we know whether they'll go ahead and prosecute.' She frowned. 'It's a worry.'

Ross's expression became serious. 'Yes, it is. Which makes it all the more surprising that your father agreed to give him a job. You've told him about the trouble he's in, haven't you?'

'Yes, of course. But my father is willing to give him a chance. He knows Finn has been working on the farm, and he's heard good things about him from the farmer.'

'I'm surprised, I'll admit. Folk around here—including your father—always thought of the McGregors as trouble—we're from the wrong side of the track, so to speak. I'd no idea that your parents would consider giving Finn the benefit of the doubt.'

She sipped her cool drink. 'I suppose they're still in two minds about things. And to be fair to Finn, he has a chance to make something of his life. Maybe that had something to do with their decision.'

'Hmm. I wonder,' His expression was brooding. 'They seem to be okay with Finn, but Jessie's been saying that they've been talking about the Old Brewery episode—she's not so sure they are able to dismiss it as something that was simply youthful folly. It seems to be on her mind quite a bit these days. She says she feels weighed down with guilt, though I've told her there's no reason for her to feel that way. It all happened a long time ago.'

'Is that what it is?' Katie frowned. 'She's been a bit

quiet lately, but she doesn't really want to talk about it when I ask her what's on her mind. I assumed it was the problems with the house that were troubling her.'

'Perhaps there's that, too.' His mouth quirked, and he seemed to be making an effort to lift the mood. 'Still, if your parents are feeling a bit more amicable towards the McGregors, maybe I'm in with a chance after all—how do you think they'd feel about me going out with their elder daughter? Would I have their blessing after all this time?'

She pretended to give it some thought. 'Oh, I wouldn't go as far as to say that. They do have certain standards…and it seems once again you're assuming I'd be in agreement with your plans…'

She was teasing him, but even though he understood that, his mouth made a crooked shape. 'Yeah. Putting that aside, I expect they've lined Josh up as a suitor for you. He has the right background, the breeding…'

'Are you serious?' Her brows lifted. 'You can't really imagine they would think that way?'

'Oh, I'm sure they want the best for their girls. I'm not convinced that I'd fit the bill.'

She reached over to him and delicately probed his shoulder with her fingers. 'That's an enormous chip you're carrying around,' she murmured. 'It must weigh you down at times.'

'Maybe you're right.' He laughed, draining his glass and getting to his feet. 'Anyway, I'd better get on with the roof while we have this fine weather. I'll go and get my tools and stuff from the car.'

'It's not safe,' she said again, still hoping to stop him from going ahead with it. 'I don't want you to go up there.'

'It'll be okay, I promise. I'm wearing rubber-soled shoes and I'll take extra care. Don't worry about it.'

It seemed she didn't have any choice but to wait while he went to gather up his tools and equipment. 'What can I do to help?' she asked when he returned. 'Shall I hold the ladder steady?'

'That sounds like a good idea.' He grinned at her. 'Don't look so anxious, Katie. It'll be fine. Tell me about the babies at the hospital. How are they doing? I didn't get the chance to check up on them yesterday.'

He started up the ladder, and she guessed he was only asking as a way of diverting her attention. 'Shouldn't you be concentrating on what you're doing, instead of listening to me?' she asked.

'I like listening to you. How's Sam? Were you able to check up on him? I know you like to follow up on your patients, so you must know something.'

'He's out of Intensive Care,' she told him. 'It looks as though the operation you did on him will provide a permanent cure for his condition. He's much stronger already, and his heart rate is normal now.'

'That's good to hear.'

She nodded. 'He's such a tiny little thing.'

'Yeah. But they're usually great fighters.' He reached the single storey roof and climbed carefully up to the apex.

Once there, he began to remove tiles, bringing them down one by one, then returning up the ladder so that he could start to fix the new ones in place. He seemed to move around with the agility of a mountain goat, but her heart was in her mouth as she watched him.

'What's happening with your little patient—the infant with chest problems?' he called down to her. 'Is her condition improving? It's very scary for everyone when a child can't breathe.'

'She's doing much better now, but we're keeping her on oxygen until she's completely stabilised.' She frowned. 'You know, Ross, I really can't answer any more questions while you're moving about up there. It's far too distracting.'

'Okay. I'm almost done here.'

She held the ladder firmly in place while he came down from the roof a while later. 'Is that it, have you finished?'

He nodded. 'I just need to hose it down to see if it's cured the problem. I'll do that and then go back into the attic to see if everything's secure.'

She sighed with relief. 'How do you know about doing this sort of thing?' she asked curiously. 'It's just not the sort of skill a doctor would be expected to have.' And yet he'd made a perfect job of it, from what she could make out.

He washed his hands at the garden tap, shaking them dry and rubbing them over his denims. 'I've picked up all sorts of useful stuff here and there over the years,' he said with a smile. 'Being in the army, you learn to survive in all sorts of conditions, so climbing on a roof is the least of my worries.'

'But you hurt yourself so badly when you were a teenager. Surely you can't have forgotten that? I certainly haven't.' Her green eyes were full of anguish at the memory. 'I was so worried when I saw you up there. I had visions of having to call for an ambulance.'

'Bless you, Katie, for caring so much.' His arms circled her, drawing her close to his tall, strong body so that she felt the comfort of his warm embrace. 'But I don't want you worrying about me. We can't have premature lines forming on that lovely face, can we?' His voice softened, became husky. 'And those sweet lips were never meant for being sad. They're made for smiling…or for kissing…'

He lowered his head and brushed his mouth over hers, gently coaxing her lips apart, softly tantalising her with his kisses and turning the blood in her veins to a fiery, molten tide. Despite all her misgivings, she realised she loved being in his arms, feeling the thunder of his heart banging against his rib cage, and with a quivery sigh she threw caution to the wind and kissed him fervently in return.

A muffled groan escaped him, and he drew her closer, holding her against him so that her soft curves melded with his powerful, muscular frame. 'This feels so good,' he murmured, his voice roughened. 'You don't know how long I've ached to hold you in my arms, to feel your beautiful body next to mine.'

His hands moved over her, gliding smoothly over every perfect curve, every line, every sensual dip and hollow, worshipping her feminine form until the heat rose in her, her body fizzed with excitement and all she wanted was to have him trail those kisses over her in endless, feverish exploration.

As if he'd read her thoughts, his lips began to trace a path over her throat, meandering leisurely along the velvet soft line of her shoulder, nudging aside the flimsy cotton shirt she was wearing. His long, caressing fingers sought out the full, ripe swell of her breast. 'Ah, Katie. I dream about you. Wanting you so much…'

Perhaps it was the heat of the afternoon sun, the faint warble of birdsong that came from nearby trees or the heady perfume of flowers that combined to subtly wear down her defences. Katie couldn't explain it, didn't want to know why all at once she could think of nothing else but being in his arms. She wanted him, needed him, would give anything to have him sweep her off her feet. It was such an overwhelming feeling, this desperate, all-consuming need.

She wasn't aware of the fingers working with cool expertise on the buttons of her shirt, and it was only when the warm breeze drifted over her bare skin that she realised he had exposed her to the elements. Her white lace-trimmed bra was no defence against his hot gaze, and in the next moment a soft sigh escaped her as his lips made a gentle foray over the pale golden flesh that spilled from the cups.

At the same time, something soft and silky brushed against the backs of her legs, and she wondered fleetingly what it might be. Ross made a ragged sound, a soft rumble in the back of his throat, and lifted his head to kiss her again. 'So beautiful,' he said, his voice low and reverent, his blue eyes as vivid as the electric-blue sky overhead.

This time the intrusion of silky fur and padding feet was far more definite as the puppy insinuated himself between them. They reluctantly broke off their embrace and looked down to see Baz, from his perch on their feet, gazing eagerly up at them. Whatever they were doing, it looked like togetherness and he wanted to join in.

Ross sighed. 'Maybe we should go into the house and find somewhere comfortable where we can be alone,' he suggested in a low, husky drawl.

Katie brushed back the loose tendrils of her hair with a shaky hand. She'd been getting out of her depth here, and now the shock of the intrusion had poured cold water on her heightened emotions. 'Perhaps we'd better not,' she said. 'I don't know what got into me. The sun must have drugged me, I think…'

She hadn't been thinking at all, or that would never have happened. She was getting in way too deep with Ross. He wanted her, but he'd admitted he couldn't give his heart to any woman because he was afraid of being hurt, and he'd never spoken of love or how he might be persuaded to set aside his reservations for her, had he?

Seeing her doubts, Ross looked down at the puppy and pulled a face. 'You have a lot to answer for, young pup.'

A brooding look came into his eyes as he turned his gaze on Katie once more.

'Perhaps I should have expected you to draw back from me. There's always going to be that class divide between us, isn't there? I shouldn't have tried to make love to you on your home territory, because it's always going to make you conscious of the difference in our backgrounds, isn't it?' A muscle flicked in his jaw. 'You'll always be the girl from the manor house, and I'll always be the hired hand. I get it. I understand.'

'No, you don't, Ross. You don't understand at all.'

'It's all right, Katie. It doesn't matter.'

He moved away from her. 'I'll get another drink and then check out the roof again.' He pulled in a deep, steadying breath. 'Where do you keep your hosepipe?'

But it did matter. Somehow, it mattered tremendously, and she thought desperately about arguing some more, to try to get her explanation across to him, but where would that lead her? Ross wanted her, but his past would always get in the way of their relationship, wouldn't it?

She stayed silent. If she reached out to him, they

would end up in the same situation all over again, and it would be a terrible mistake, because Ross couldn't possibly be the man for her...could he?

CHAPTER EIGHT

'DO YOU WANT any more coffee or shall I start to clear away?' Jessie held the coffee pot aloft for Katie to see.

'No, thanks. I've had all I want.'

'Okay.' Jessie glanced at her watch. 'I need to get a move on. I'm supposed to be organising a day out for a little birthday girl and her friends today. There'll be tractor rides, messing about in the hay barn and all sorts of things that I need to supervise. Ending with a birthday lunch in the upper hall, of course, and what's the betting someone will eat too much cake and be sick? That happened at the last two parties.'

Katie pulled a face. 'I'm glad I don't have to deal with that—it's been bad enough lately, with Baz being sick off and on.' She frowned. 'I can't think what's causing it. I've been really careful with his food, and he certainly seems to be healthy enough. The vet said he was doing really well when he had his last lot of vaccinations. It's very odd.'

She didn't know how she was going to explain it to Ross and Finn. They were both concerned about him. Her mind veered away from thoughts of Ross. She was too churned up inside emotionally to be able to think straight when it came to anything to do with him.

'You're right. It's a puzzle to know what's going on.'

Jessie started to clear the breakfast table, and glanced out of the window to where Baz was playing in the garden with the boy from next door. He'd taken to coming around regularly to play with the puppy. 'I don't know what's been going on out there,' she remarked. 'Jack's looking a bit concerned.'

'Is he?' Katie brought her mind back to everyday matters and followed her gaze. 'I'll go and find out what the problem is. It's about time for Baz to come in anyway. I have to be at work soon.'

She went out into the garden and walked onto the lawn where seven-year-old Jack was frowning as he studied the flowerbeds. 'Is something wrong, Jack?' she asked. There was no sign of Baz, until she caught sight of the tip of his tail waving above a curtain of ferns.

'He's been sick again,' he told her worriedly. 'It's making me feel a bit sick as well.'

'Oh, dear. You do look a bit pale.' Katie put a comforting arm around him. 'Perhaps you'd better go back home and tell your mum about it. It might help if you lie down for a bit until your tummy settles.'

He nodded, and she slowly walked him back to his house. 'You'll be able to see Baz later,' she told him.

Jack's father hadn't left for work yet. His car was still in the drive, and as Katie approached the house she could hear sounds of raised voices from inside.

'There were three of those small pork pies in the fridge this morning and now there are only two,' Jack's mother was saying. 'I wanted them for this evening. I don't understand it—I can't keep track of anything just lately. It's as though I'm going mad. Things keep going missing.'

Katie glanced at Jack. That, at least, answered a question in her mind. The child was biting his lip and seemed reluctant to go indoors. 'It'll be all right, Jack,' she told him. 'I'll tell your mother that you're not feeling well. Okay?' She urged him forward and knocked on the kitchen door.

'Jack's feeling a bit under the weather,' she said, when her neighbour answered the door. 'I think he might need to lie down for a while. I'm sorry I can't stop, but I have to be at work soon.'

Her neighbour smiled. 'Thanks for bringing him back, Katie. I'll take care of him.' She felt the child's forehead with the back of her hand and led him away, carefully closing the door.

Katie walked back to the house, calling Baz as she went. He trotted beside her, apparently recovered from his illness and eager to find his basket and his toys.

'I think I know why Baz is being sick,' Katie told Jessie. 'I've a feeling Jack's been feeding him pork pies and all sorts of goodies.'

'Oh, heavens!' Jessie looked at him and stroked his head as he settled down in his basket. 'You poor little thing.'

Katie left for work a short time later, and sought out her first patient in one of the treatment rooms. She was a little disturbed to find Ross already in there with the child, but she put on a professional front and prepared to greet him in what she hoped was at least a friendly manner.

They had been cautious around one another ever since that day when he'd come over to the house, but they had to work together, and she was trying to be as normal as she could around him. It was hard, but as long as she kept their conversations strictly to work matters, she felt she could just about handle the situation.

He was sitting with the child's mother, who supported

her two-year-old daughter on her lap while Ross held an oxygen mask in front of the toddler's nose and mouth. The mother was comforting the child, who was lethargic but clearly distressed.

'Hi, there.' Ross introduced Katie to the mother, adding, 'Dr Brechan will be looking after Alice. She'll take good care of her.'

Katie nodded, and smiled at the young woman. 'I'll listen to her chest and try to find out what's going on in there.' She could see that the little girl was struggling for air, pulling on her chest and abdominal muscles to help with her breathing. When she'd finished her examination and looked at the child's fingers and toes, she found there was a faint blue tinge about them.

'We'll admit her to the paediatric ward,' she said, 'and in the meantime we'll keep her on humidified oxygen with nebulised adrenaline.' She noted the medications down on the chart. 'And we'll give her corticosteroids, which should help ease things for her.'

Ross nodded agreement, telling the mother, 'I think it will help if you loosen her clothing a little. She's quite feverish, and we need to bring her temperature down to make her more comfortable.' He stood up, passing the oxygen mask to the woman, and then he began to apply pads to the girl's chest, so that she could be linked up to the monitors. 'You'll be all right, sweetheart,' he said softly to the little girl. 'I know you're feeling miserable right now, but we'll look after you.'

Katie watched him, touched by his gentleness. It was a wonderful thing to see, this strong man showing such a tender side, and it brought a lump to her throat. She had to drag her gaze away from him, though, and busy herself with the job in hand, taking a blood sample for testing and making sure that the medications were started right away.

Later, when they were sure that the little girl was less agitated and all the treatment protocols were in place, they left the mother and child in the care of a nurse.

Ross walked with Katie to the nurses' station. There was silence between them for a while, but then he asked, 'Have you seen anything of Finn lately? I heard things had gone wrong at home and he was thinking of packing a bag and leaving. I wondered if he'd asked you and Jessie to put him up?'

'Oh dear, are things that bad for him at home?' she said, looking at him worriedly. 'He came to the house yesterday as usual and took Baz for a walk. I didn't have too much time to stop and talk with him, but he did mention that his father was making life difficult for him. He said nothing he did was right. I told him parents and teenagers often have problems understanding one another and I thought they should try and sort things out between them.'

'Hmm. That's easier said than done.' Ross made a face. 'When I think back to my childhood, it's like history repeating itself.'

'All the more reason to nip it in the bud, don't you think? Or is Finn to end up leaving home and joining the army in order to escape, the way you did? What will his mother think of that? She's been ill—she must be worried sick by all this. And I know you're trying to help him, but I don't think it will make things easier for her if you encourage him to move in with you. He should be dealing with his problems, not running away from them.'

'So you think I'm to blame for the way he's acting?' His jaw tightened.

'I didn't say that. I just think there must be a way around the problem.'

His expression was cynical. 'You have no idea how the other half live, have you? Everything is straightforward for you, your family is always there for you, strong and supportive and going the way they've always gone, quietly and traditionally, following years of good breeding and high standards. Not every family works that way, you know.'

She sent him an exasperated look. 'Does it have to come back to that every time, with you? My family's really not much different to any other. We have our ups and downs, the same as anyone else.'

He shrugged. 'Maybe it's my background that's to blame after all, then. We're the odd ones out.'

Katie bit back a retort as Shona appeared with a patient's file, urging her to attend a small boy who appeared to be suffering from an infected joint. 'I'll be right there,' Katie told her.

'And there's a youth coming in by ambulance,' Shona told Ross. 'He has some kind of heart rhythm complaint. The paramedics think it might have something to do with drug taking.'

'I'll go and see to him,' Ross murmured. He went off towards the ambulance bay, and after that Katie only saw him briefly throughout the day as their paths crossed intermittently while they were treating their patients.

At the end of her shift, she put on her jacket and readied herself for the journey home. A phone call stopped her as she headed for the main doors, and she paused for a while to listen to what Jessie had to say.

'I won't be home till late this evening,' Jessie told her, 'so don't worry about the evening meal—just fix something for yourself. Josh is going to come over to my new house with me to sort out a problem with the builders.

'I think they're messing me about, working for a while on my house and then leaving it to go and sort out someone else's property, only they keep asking for interim payments without doing the work.'

Katie frowned. 'I'm glad you have Josh to help you deal with that. No wonder the alterations have taken longer than you expected. It'll be good if you can work it all out.'

'It will. I've been lucky that you've been able to put me up for the last few weeks, but I thought I'd be moving out long before this.'

'Don't worry about it,' Katie said with a smile. 'You know you can stay as long as you like.'

'Thanks. You're an angel.' Katie could hear the smile in her voice, but then Jessie's tone changed, as she said quickly, 'And there's another problem...young Jack from next door has gone missing. His parents have been looking for him for the last two or three hours, but they can't find him anywhere. They told me they'd been arguing about something, and they think Jack took fright and went off.'

'But he can't have gone far, surely?' Katie's brows drew together, and she looked up to see that Ross had come to join her by the doors. He paused, ready to key in the pass code, but waited when he saw that something appeared to be wrong. She mouthed silently to him that Jack had run away and he watched her in concern.

'I don't know,' Jessie answered. 'I joined in the hunt for him, and they contacted all his friends' families, but we came up empty. They've called in the police. Freya's out of her mind with worry. On top of all this, she says he's not been too well today. Nothing specific, just that he had a tummy ache and he's been feeling sick and wouldn't eat anything.'

'Yes, he said he felt sick this morning. His poor mother must be frantic, waiting at home for news. I think I'll join in the search if they haven't found him by the time I get home.'

'I thought you might want to do that. I expect Josh and I will join in as well once we've been over to the house.' Jessica rang off, saying, 'I'll see you later, Katie. I hope they find him.'

'So do I.' Katie pushed her phone down into the pocket of her jacket.

'It sounds bad,' Ross commented. 'Where will you look for him that they haven't tried already?'

'I'm not sure.' She lifted her shoulders in a helpless gesture. 'They've concentrated the search locally so far, but I guess they'll widen it now. I know Jack's fascinated by the offshore island. We walked together with Baz along the strait when the tide was out a couple of evenings ago, but I told him he shouldn't go there on his own because it was dangerous at high tide, and I'm sure his mother would have told him the same thing.

'Then again, he might have gone into the woods to hide. I suppose. I imagine they'll be doing an extensive search there.'

He nodded. 'Look, I have to go to an important meeting right now, but afterwards, if there's still no news about him, I'll come and help with the search.'

'Okay. Perhaps I'll see you later.'

'Yes. But let's hope it's all sorted out before then.'

Katie drove home, her mind full of chaotic thoughts. There was anxiety for young Jack, but it was tinged with anguish over her relationship with Ross. He was talking to her as though all was well, but there wasn't the same intimacy in his manner towards her as there had been before, and she was beginning to realise she didn't like that at all.

Jack's mother, Freya, was white-faced and tearful when Katie saw her a short time later. 'I don't know what can have happened to Jack, Katie. I keep thinking, what if he went to the loch?' She wrung her hands in despair. 'I don't know what to do. I want to join in the search, but I have to stay here and look after the little one and wait in case he comes back.' She clutched Jack's small sister close to her as though she was afraid she, too, might disappear.

Katie gave her a hug. 'I'll take Baz out with me and we'll see if we have any luck,' she said. 'Do you have anything that Jack has worn recently? If Baz gets a scent, he's really good at following the trail.'

Freya found a sweater that Jack had been wearing earlier that day, and a short time later Katie put on her jacket and went outside with Baz. She gave him the sweater to sniff and he wandered around the garden a few times, before apparently picking up the little boy's scent on the path.

His tail wagged in excitement and he pulled on his leash, anxious to be off. For once, instead of making him walk to heel, Katie let him lead the way, but as they hurried away from the house and along the coastal ridge, she began to wonder if this was all a mistake.

After all, the boxer was still a puppy, only a few months old, with no scent training as such. Every now and again he became distracted, pausing to examine a hillock, or a fascinating clump of heather, and she began to think they might be setting out on a wild-goose chase.

Then he headed for the narrow strait that linked this island with the small islet to the north, where the only inhabitants were grey herons that nested in the woodland by the loch and roe deer and other species of wildlife.

Katie looked uneasily at the encroaching tide. Twice a day the sea crept in and covered the strait, leaving the islet cut off for several hours from the main island. Watching the channel slowly become narrower, she had a horrible feeling that they were fast running out of time.

'Are you sure you know where you're taking me,' she asked the puppy, 'or is this another adventure trip for you? We have to find Jack…hopefully before the tide comes in.' She let him sniff the sweater once more.

His tail wagged happily and he pulled Katie further along the sandy passage.

She would give it another fifteen minutes, she promised herself. That would be enough for a quick look around, and then she would start the return journey. With any luck, she would make it back home before the sea covered the strait.

Baz forged on ahead, plunging along the heather-clad hillside and into a valley cut through by a fast-running burn. Then they came to a small copse and he stopped for a moment or two, as though he had lost the trail.

Katie looked around in despair. 'Is this it?' she said softly. 'Where do we go now?' She crouched down and stroked the dog's silky ears. 'You've done your best, I know. You thought you could find Jack, but it looks as though he isn't here.'

She sighed. 'We'd best go home. It'll be dark before too long, and the tide will cut us off if we don't hurry.' She didn't know why she was talking to the puppy. He couldn't understand a word she said, but his ears had pricked up at the sound of Jack's name.

He nosed around in the undergrowth for a while,

and then started to explore the rotted trunk of a tree that must have fallen during a winter storm. She let out the leash to its longest extent so that he could roam a little further, and after a second or two he disappeared from sight. He yelped excitedly a couple of times and she frowned. Had he found something?

She walked around the fallen tree, picking her way over tangled roots and leaf mould. The bole of the tree was massive, hollowed out in parts where it had decayed, and at first she couldn't make out what she was seeing, because the clothing was dark and matched the colour of the bark.

Then she gasped as realisation dawned and shock rooted her to the spot. Jack lay huddled in the shelter of the tree, beads of perspiration covering his brow, his breath coming in short rasps.

'Oh, Jack, thank heaven. You're safe now, sweetheart. I've got you.' She quickly knelt down beside him and gently cradled him in her arms. He winced in pain as he turned towards her.

'Where does it hurt, Jack? Can you show me?'

He moved his hand weakly over the right side of his abdomen and her heart sank. The boy was sick, and she had the horrible feeling that it wasn't just a simple stomach upset that ailed him.

She carefully slipped off her jacket and wrapped it around the boy. Then she took out her mobile phone and dialled the number for the police and ambulance. There was no dial tone and, in shock, she stared blankly at the screen. She couldn't get a signal. What should she do?

Her heart began to thump wildly, and she looked around in dismay. They were out here in the wilderness, and Jack was far too ill to walk anywhere. There was no way she could get him across the strait before the tide came in and covered everything in its path. They were stuck here on this small island.

Her mind clouded briefly. What was she to do? If only Ross could be here by her side. She missed him. With him around, she felt that anything was possible. They would be safe with him, she was sure of it. He would know what to do.

Most of all, right now, she wanted to feel his arms around her, holding her close.

Only he wasn't here and she couldn't even talk to him on the phone. He was back at home, and it looked as though she and Jack were set to be together for a long, lonely night. Despair washed over her.

CHAPTER NINE

THE SKY WAS overcast now, ominously grey and threatening rain, and the wind had built up, blowing in heavy gusts that tossed Katie's hair this way and that, and struck a chill through her so that she began to shiver. Baz was lying at her feet, content to rest after his long trek, his head supported on his front paws.

She looked down at Jack, tucking her jacket around him. He hadn't been saying very much, simply lying there for the most part with his eyes closed. Now, though, he muttered gruffly, 'I'm going to be sick again.' And he turned his head to one side and vomited into the undergrowth. He cried out with pain from the exertion, and when it was over Katie helped make him more comfortable, wiping his mouth with a tissue from her bag.

His fair hair was damp with perspiration, and she was afraid that his fever was getting worse. Somehow she had to get him to shelter, out of the way of the storm that was brewing.

Exhausted, he settled back in her arms once more. 'I'm going to be in trouble with Mum and Dad,' he said wearily, looking thoroughly miserable.

'Why would you think that? I'm sure your parents are very worried about you.'

He shook his head. 'I took a piece of cherry pie from the fridge,' he said. 'I was going to give it to Baz, but I ate it myself and it made me poorly. They'll be cross with me.'

'Is that why you ran away?'

He nodded, and Katie smiled. 'I don't think they'll be cross, Jack,' she told him. 'I don't think it was the pie that made you sick.' She laid a hand lightly on his forehead, brushing away his damp hair. 'I think you have an infection of some kind. It's probably nothing to do with what you've eaten.'

She looked around. 'But we need to get you under some kind of cover,' she said quietly. 'I think there's a bothy somewhere around here where we might be able to get out of this cold wind. If I could just remember where to find it.'

She frowned. Ross would know where it was. He'd mentioned it to her once when they had been talking about the surrounding islands, and he'd said he'd stayed in the cottage one night when he'd been a teenager and he'd left home after an argument with his father.

She hadn't been to this place in a long time, and she racked her brain, trying to think where the stone-built cottage was located. It had been made for this very purpose—to shelter any unfortunate souls who were unlucky enough to find themselves stranded out here. But where was it?

She peered through the trees, trying to make out shapes through the descending gloom. There was a rough-hewn path winding its way through the copse that continued to the meadow beyond, and in the recesses of her mind she saw the image of a white-painted building that dominated the hillside.

'You can't see it until you come out of the copse and

walk on a bit,' Ross had said, 'but once you get up there it's a wonderful experience. It overlooks the valley, and on a clear day you can see for miles around.'

'Okay, Jack,' she murmured. 'I'm going to lift you up and carry you. I know you're in pain, but I promise I'll be as careful as I can be.'

She looped Baz's leash over her wrist and cautiously lifted Jack in her arms, trying to disturb him as little as possible. Even so, he moaned softly with the movement.

They followed the path for five minutes or so before she stopped to take a breather, leaning against a sturdy oak and using a low branch for support. She daren't put the child down for fear of hurting him, but her arms were aching under the strain of carrying him and she hoped it wouldn't be too long before they reached the bothy.

Then, faintly, in the distance, she thought she heard someone calling her name. Her eyes widened. It wasn't possible, was it? Could it be?

The sound came closer, became louder, and she called back, 'I'm here. Ross, we're over here.'

A moment later she saw him striding over the rise of the hill and her heart swelled with relief. He was here. Her prayers had been answered.

'How did you know where to find me?' she asked, her face lighting up with joy at the sight of him. He was wearing a backpack, and she guessed he had come prepared for anything. 'The phones are out—I tried calling for help but there's no signal.'

'I know, I've been trying to get in touch with you. Freya told me you'd set off with Baz, and I had the feeling you might head this way. No one had seen you for the last hour so I decided to try my luck.'

'But surely the tide is in by now? Did you come by

boat? Could we get back that way? We need to get Jack to a hospital as soon as possible.'

'I borrowed the motorboat, but there's no chance of using it to get back. The sea's way too choppy. It took everything I had to keep it on course to get here.' He reached for Jack. 'Here, let me take him.'

'Thanks. But go carefully, he's in an awful lot of pain. He's been sick twice.'

He nodded. 'Okay. I have him.' He looked along the path. 'I guessed you might be heading for the bothy. It's not far from here, just over the next rise.'

The wind howled around them as they set off, and Katie bent her head against it, shivering as they set off up the path.

'You should have my coat,' Ross said, coming to a halt and getting ready to set the child down so that he could take off his soft leather jacket.

'No, don't disturb him,' she said in a low voice. 'I'm afraid he might have appendicitis, and the last thing we want is for the appendix to rupture. We need to keep him as still as possible.' If she was right in her diagnosis, the appendix had become obstructed, and inflammation would have set in soon afterwards. 'It's not far now, anyway. I can see the bothy from here.'

They reached the building a few minutes later, and Katie held the door open and lit the oil lamps while Ross laid Jack down on one of the camp beds on the sleeping platform. Katie let Baz off his leash and he padded around the room, exploring his new surroundings.

There was just one large L-shaped main room, with all the facilities they might need for an overnight stay, including a wood-burning stove and a supply of cold water.

'Would you bring one of the lamps over here, Katie,

please?' Ross said. 'I'm going to examine the lad to see what we can do for him.' He laid his backpack down on the platform and as he opened it Katie realised that it contained a complete medical kit.

'Oh, you came prepared,' she said. She might have known Ross wouldn't leave anything to chance. 'I should have thought of that,' she added, with a stab of guilt, 'but after talking to him this morning, I'd assumed it was just a stomach upset—it didn't occur to me that he was seriously ill.'

'I spoke to Freya and something she said about his symptoms during the day alerted me so I thought it best to be on the safe side.'

She laid a hand on his arm. 'Ross, I'm so glad you're here. You can't imagine what a relief it was for me to see you coming up the hill.'

He gave her a quick, warm embrace. 'I had to come, Katie. I was afraid you'd be cut off by the tide and I thought you might need some help.' He smiled and began to take off his jacket. 'Here, put this around your shoulders. You look half-frozen.'

'Thanks.' He slid the coat over her, and immediately she felt the warmth that came from his body heat and the faint smell of soft, supple leather filled her nostrils. 'I'll see if I can light the stove,' she said. 'There are some matches on the shelf. That should soon warm the place up.'

'That'll be good.'

'We need to find some way to let them know back home that we've found him,' Katie said, trying her phone once more. There was still no signal and she sighed in frustration. 'His parents will be frantic with worry.'

'Yes, I've been thinking about that.' He began to

make a gentle but careful examination of the little boy, while Katie lit the fire and set a kettle of water to boil on the primitive camping stove. There were packets of tea and coffee in a cupboard, along with dried milk, sugar and biscuits. At least they wouldn't go hungry or thirsty.

She went over to Ross and Jack and set down a cup of coffee on the shelf beside Ross. 'How's he doing?' she asked in a low voice. 'It *is* appendicitis, isn't it? He looks calmer, though—did you give him a painkiller?'

'Yes, it is, and I've given him a strong analgesic and anti-inflammatory medication, as well as something to bring his temperature down and an anti-emetic to stop him being sick.'

'What about antibiotics? Do you have them in your kit?' It looked a pretty comprehensive set-up, the kind that emergency doctors carried around with them when they were working on immediate care away from the hospital.

'I do. I'm going to give him an intravenous antibiotic now—I think he's looking dehydrated, though, so we need to get a fluid line in.'

'I can do that for you.' She was already pulling on surgical gloves ready for the procedure. 'Take a break. You haven't stopped since you set out across the strait, have you? Drink your coffee. I'll take care of Jack.'

'Thanks.' He took a quick swallow of the hot liquid then put down his cup and stood up. 'I'm going to see if I can start a fire outside. The police will probably be getting up a helicopter to help with the search and they might see it and put two and two together.'

'That's a good idea. There's plenty of kindling by the stove. Here, take your jacket. I'm warm enough now, and you'll need it outside.'

'Okay.' He shrugged it on and went to gather up an armful of firewood before leaving the cottage.

Katie quickly put a cannula in Jack's arm, securing it in place and setting up a fluid line. Then she gave him the antibiotic he needed to counteract the infection from the appendicitis. If only they could get him to hospital, he could undergo emergency surgery. If not, there was the risk that the appendix could rupture, spreading dangerous infection throughout his body, leading to life-threatening septicaemia.

A waft of cold air hit her as the door opened and Ross came into the bothy once more. 'How did you get on?' she asked, stripping off her gloves.

'All right, I think. It's a pretty good blaze—as long as the rain holds off, we stand a chance that it will be seen. I'll go and look at it again in a while to make sure it's still burning.'

He came over to her and looked down at Jack. 'He's asleep,' he said, his expression softening. 'That's a blessing.'

'Yes, it is. It's hard to believe he went through all that pain and daren't tell his parents—he thought he'd brought it on himself, and they would be cross with him. Poor little thing…the world must seem a strange place for a seven-year-old.'

'I guess so. At least he's comfortable for now.'

She nodded and stood up. 'Why don't you come over to the stove and try to get warm? There's some food here, too. I hadn't realised it until now, but I'm absolutely starving. I haven't eaten anything since lunch.'

'Neither have I.' He joined her, basking in the heat from the stove for a minute or two, and then he went to inspect the cupboard where the food was stored. 'Biscuits, packets of dried soup, tinned fruit. That's a feast.

Whoever stocked this cabin deserves a medal. I brought chocolate with me, too, so we're well set up.'

'Chocolate?' She said the word in an almost reverent tone and slid her arms around him. 'You're my most favourite person in all the world,' she said with a wide, mischievous smile. 'Did I ever tell you how much I love chocolate?'

'Well, now, I don't think you did.' A devilish gleam came into his eyes. 'So, exactly how much do you like it? What's it worth to you?'

She smiled. 'Depends what you're asking.'

'Mmm. Let me see, I'll have to think about that.' His eyes darkened, and his arms circled her waist so that he had her captured in a warm embrace. 'Maybe a kiss will do…just for starters…'

'For starters?' She lifted her face to him in teasing expectation. 'What comes afterwards?'

'I haven't worked that out yet.' His mouth curved. 'Let's start with a kiss and we'll see where we go from there, shall we?'

She didn't need any persuading. In the space of a few hours her emotions had rocketed through the whole range from desolation to delight, and having him here with her after the trauma of finding herself stranded was everything she'd dreamed of.

So, when he swooped down and tenderly claimed her lips, she was right there with him, eager for his kisses and desperate to feel his hard body next to hers.

She reached up to him, letting her fingers explore the strong sinews of his neck and shoulders and running her fingers through his hair. She loved the way his arms tightened around her, the way his muscular thighs tangled with hers. Their bodies meshed, her soft, feminine curves melding with his powerful masculine frame, and she clung to him, wanting this moment to go on for ever.

It couldn't, of course, not with a sick little boy lying just a few feet away from them. Ross knew it, too, and after a few moments of bliss they both came back down to earth with a shared look of regret.

'Think of that as a down payment,' he murmured huskily, letting his hand rest lightly on her hip as though he couldn't bear to drag himself away from her.

'You're saying I'm in your debt?' she said with a lift of a finely shaped brow. 'Hmm. We'll see. Maybe after you taste my chicken soup you might find that *you* owe *me*.'

He chuckled. 'Interesting,' he commented. 'Either way, I'm up for it.'

She sent him a look from under her lashes. 'Somehow I thought you might be.' It was just banter, but she loved being with him this way, feeling at ease with one another and keeping the outside world at bay. She took a packet of soup down from the cupboard and hunted out a saucepan. 'I'll rehydrate this,' she said, adding water to the pan. 'Supper will be ready in about five minutes.'

At the mention of supper Baz's ears pricked up and he trotted over to her to see if there was any food to be had.

Ross smiled, playfully tickling the dog's ears. 'Time enough for me to go and check the fire,' he said. 'I haven't heard any aircraft flying overhead, but there's still a chance they might widen the search. I hope they do, for Jack's sake.' He grimaced. 'Appendixes rupture when they reach a certain point, and from the amount of pain he was in, I think he's almost there.'

She nodded. It didn't bear thinking about. Jack needed to be in hospital, in Theatre, having his appendix removed.

Jack mumbled in his sleep, and she went over to him. His face was hot, and when she took his temperature she realised that his fever was running out of control, despite the medication.

She found a clean cloth in Ross's backpack and soaked it in cold water. Then she carefully wrung it out and laid it on the boy's forehead. It should help a little.

'Is there a problem?' Ross said, coming back into the room. 'Has he taken a turn for the worse?'

'He's burning up,' she answered softly. 'We need to cool him down.' She filled a bowl with cool water and placed it on the sleeping platform next to the child.

'I'll see to it,' Ross told her, finding another cloth and moistening it so that he could bathe the boy's neck and chest. 'You can concentrate on the food, if you like.'

'Okay.'

She served up the meal a few minutes later, and they took it in turns to look after Jack, while eating the simple fare. It was surprisingly good, wholesome soup that warmed them through and through, and an apricot dessert provided a sweet, delicious finish.

Jack was still sleeping while Katie cleared away the dishes and washed them at the sink. He was slightly less flushed now, and that was a relief to her. Ross kept an eye on him, checking the fluid bag to make sure he was being adequately hydrated.

'When this is over, we'll have to come back here to restock the supplies we've used,' Katie murmured, coming to sit beside him on the platform.

Ross nodded. 'I can see to that. They order in a good supply of kindling at McAskie's for their own wood-burning stoves, so I expect the landlord will let me buy some from him. I doubt I'll have time to gather any locally.'

'I expect you'll be leaving there before too long, won't you? Are you ready to move into your new house yet?'

'Just about. Another day or so and the furniture should pretty much be in place by then.'

'So this will be your last weekend at McAskie's?' Katie frowned. 'I heard they're holding a barbecue. That sounds like fun. I know Jessie's looking forward to it.'

He grinned. 'Yes, she said she doesn't have to work this weekend and she's planning on letting her hair down and having a really good time.'

'You and she get on well, don't you? She's always talking about you.'

'Is she? Yes, I like Jessie a lot. I've always liked her. She's been to the pub quite a lot lately, so we've had a chance to catch up on old times.'

'And you'll be there, at the barbecue, too, will you?'

'Of course. I have to be there. We're holding a charity fair in the grounds to raise money for the new nurse-led minor injuries unit.' He raised a dark brow. 'Didn't you read the memo? I sent it to everyone. We want as many of the staff who can make it to be there, and we've advertised it locally. There should be a good turnout.'

'Oh, I see. No, I didn't see the memo. It must have passed me by.' She pressed her lips together briefly. 'You're determined to go ahead with the unit, then? I wondered if you'd put your plans on hold for a while.'

'I don't believe in delaying tactics. You know me better than that, don't you?' He gave her a searching look. 'So, will you be there?'

She thought about it. Now that she'd had time to come down from the high of being in his arms, she wasn't so sure it was such a good idea to be so involved with him out of work. Wasn't she treading on thin ice and setting herself up for a tragic fall? He'd made it clear enough that all he wanted was a light-hearted relationship, for them to have some fun together, as he'd put it. The problem was, she wanted much more than that.

'Maybe.' The idea of spending the day with him was more than tempting, but she simply didn't trust herself around him. Look what had happened here just a short time ago. Before she knew it, things could spiral out of control.

He seemed perplexed. 'You can't still be annoyed with me for wanting to change things, can you? I know I took the job you wanted, Katie, but you're my right-hand woman, you know that, don't you? I thought we could work together on this. I want you to be there.'

Did he want her there to help out or to be with him? She wasn't sure, and suddenly she was afraid to ask in case he gave the wrong answer. She was torn by so many conflicting emotions.

He must have taken her silence to mean that she needed more persuading, because he said with a gleam in his eyes, 'And, besides, you owe me. After all, you did eat the chocolate, didn't you?'

She sucked in her breath and then relaxed. 'Just a teensy bit,' she said, making a minuscule show of the amount with her fingers. 'Don't imagine you can hold me to that.'

He chuckled, but just then Jack moaned in pain and they both went to him, any hint of amusement dissolving rapidly into thin air.

'It's all right, Jack, we're here.' She took his pulse and turned to Ross with a worried look. 'His heart's racing,' she said in a whisper. 'We're losing the battle here. It's too soon to give him any more anti-inflammatory medication, and the antibiotics will have barely kicked in…'

'I can give him more pain medication. That should reduce the stress a bit.' He glanced at his watch. 'I'd have thought they'd be over here looking for him by now.'

As he spoke, the drone of an aircraft sounded overhead, and Ross hurried outside, taking with him a white towel to wave as a flag. Katie sat beside Jack and waited, hoping it was the rescue team. They had to have come for him...

Some ten minutes later Jack was safely secured inside the helicopter. Katie was relieved to see that there was basic medical equipment on board, and she quickly placed pads on Jack's chest and connected him to the monitors.

The pilot sent a message over the radio to let the search party know that the child had been found, and Katie heard the gasps of relief as the news was conveyed to the waiting parents.

Baz wasn't at all sure what was going on, but it must have seemed like a new adventure to him because he sniffed everything and everyone until he eventually settled himself contentedly by Ross's feet. Very shortly after that they were airborne and heading for the hospital, where a surgical team would be ready and waiting for them.

Katie looked out of the window, watching as the white-painted building gradually faded from view. She was almost sorry to be leaving the cottage behind. For a short time back there she'd been intensely happy, wrapped up in Ross's arms, and this surely had to be more than just an infatuation or a fleeting obsession.

She cared about him deeply, was desperate to have him near, and now she was wondering how she would live without him. Somehow, over these last few weeks, she had grown to love him, but she had no real idea whether he felt the same way about her. Was it possible that he could love her, or was she just another girl to him, another light-hearted fling as far as he was concerned?

She had no idea what the future held for her. Would Ross be part of it?

At last the helicopter started the descent to the hospital's helipad. By now, it was the early hours of the morning, and except for the landing lights there was darkness all around.

Jack moaned softly, his face contorted with pain, and Katie quickly checked the monitors. Ross exchanged glances with her, his expression grim.

'I was hoping it wouldn't come to this,' he said. 'His vital signs are getting worse, and that can only mean one thing.'

'The appendix has ruptured.' Katie spoke in a soft undertone, not wanting to alarm the boy in any way, and Ross nodded.

'The surgical team are ready and waiting for him. I want to scrub in and follow through with him in Theatre,' he said as they made their way to the medics waiting for them.

'I guessed you might want to do that.' She knew he wanted to be with Jack right to the end. They were both intensely concerned that the boy should come through this episode safely.

The medics quickly transferred Jack to a trolley and hurried away with him to Theatre. Ross followed, giving an up-to-date account of Jack's medical history along the way.

'The boy's parents are in the waiting room,' a nurse told Katie. 'They're extremely anxious about him.'

'That's understandable. I'll go and talk to them,' she

said. She wasn't looking forward to that meeting—how could she tell her neighbours that their little boy was very ill, in pain, and in danger of his life? Peritonitis was an infection of the tissue that lined the abdomen and the abdominal organs, and if it ran out of control it could lead to septicaemia and organ failure.

Jack's condition was deteriorating with every minute that passed. Once the appendix burst, the infection, which had been relatively contained up to this point, would spread rapidly through the child's body. It was an extremely worrying situation, but Katie forced herself to stay calm and did her best to reassure Freya and her husband that everything possible was being done.

'The surgeon will take out the appendix and put a tube in his abdomen to drain the infection,' she told them. 'When Jack's out of Theatre, if they have managed to catch it in time, he'll return to the ward and be put on antibiotics. However there is a chance that the appendix has burst, which means that he'll go straight to the intensive care unit.'

'Katie, thank you so much for finding him and looking after him,' Freya said, grasping her hands in a warm embrace. 'We've been so worried. All sorts of things were going through our minds—but we never dreamed he was so ill.'

'I know. It must have been a terrible time for you, and I'm so sorry I couldn't get in touch with you sooner.' Katie gently squeezed her hands in return. 'But it was actually Baz that found him. He knew exactly where to go and he kept on following the trail until we reached him.'

Her mouth curved as she recalled the puppy's eagerness. Finn had come over to take care of Baz as soon as she had rung him, which meant that she could stay at the hospital until Jack was safely out of surgery. She wasn't going anywhere until she knew that was over.

'He's a great dog, isn't he, Katie?' Finn had said, his eyes shining with pride. 'I knew he was special.'

'You're right, Finn. He's the best.' Katie had smiled, and had watched Finn walk off with the puppy, who had eagerly watched Finn's every move, his tail wagging non-stop. He knew he had done something good because of all the fuss he was getting.

Jack was in Theatre for over an hour, but eventually Ross came to find her, taking her to one side while the surgeon showed the boy's parents into his office where they could talk for a while.

Ross looked pleased to see her. 'I'm glad you're here,' he said quietly. 'I wondered if you might have gone home by now. It's very late, and you've had a long, difficult day, one way and another.'

She shook her head. 'So have you. I couldn't leave, not until I knew he'd come through this all right. How did it go?' She studied him. He looked weary, his face reflecting the strain of the last few hours, and for a moment or two, she feared the worst.

'The appendix had ruptured. It didn't look too good to begin with, but we managed to clean out most of the infected matter. I'm hoping that with a strong antibiotic regime and good nursing care, he should start to recover. In the meantime, he's sedated and we're keeping a close eye on him. We can only wait and see what happens now.'

'You did everything you could,' she said softly. 'I hate to think what might have happened if you hadn't come after us. I had no medical kit, nothing that would be any use…'

He draped an arm around her. 'I had to find you, to

make sure you were okay. I wouldn't have rested until I'd done that.' He gazed into her eyes. 'Come on, I'll see you home. I expect we can cadge a lift with the paramedics.'

'All right.'

He was quiet on the journey home, and she guessed he was still thinking about the boy's close call. Jack's illness had affected both of them, all the more so because he wasn't just a patient, a stranger. They both knew this little boy and were friendly with him. Katie had often watched him play with Baz and had smiled at their antics. She even had photos of them on her mobile phone.

'Try to get a good night's sleep,' Ross murmured as the paramedics dropped her off outside her house. 'I'll see you tomorrow.' Then he reached down and kissed her gently on the mouth.

'Goodnight, Ross.' Even though it was brief and over with before she could get used to it, her mouth burned from the searing contact of that kiss. It warmed her through and through, and she hugged the sweetness of it to her as she let herself into the house.

She was startled when Jessie met her in the hallway. 'You came home with Ross,' Jessie said. 'What happened? Did you find Jack?' She hesitated for a second or two, frowning. 'Did I see things right? Did Ross actually kiss you just now?'

Katie winced. 'Whoa. Slow down a bit. Which question do you want me to answer first?'

'Did you find Jack? It's been all over the village that you went across the strait and must have been stranded there. I guessed Ross must have been with you.'

'News travels fast around here, doesn't it?' Katie nodded. 'Yes, we found him.' She explained about the

appendicitis and added, 'He's in Intensive Care, and
Jack's parents are there with him.'

'I'm glad about that.' Jessie eyed her cautiously as
they walked into the sitting room. 'So what was going
on with you and Ross? He kissed you…'

'Yes, he did.'

Jessie's gaze was penetrating. 'Is something going
on with you two? Something I should know about?'

'Um, maybe.' Katie pulled in a breath. 'I really care
about him, Jessie. I think I'm in love with him.'

Jessie's reaction wasn't quite what she might have expected. Her sister was silent for a moment, taking it in,
and then she said in an odd voice, 'So it's serious, then?
You've been so careful not to let your guard down ever
since your ex. Does Ross feel the same way?'

'Uh, I don't know. I'm not sure.' Was it possible
for Ross to ever give his heart to a woman? After all,
he, too, was afraid of being hurt, and the demons that
haunted him went right back to his childhood.

She gave her sister a concerned look. 'What's wrong,
Jessie? You seem troubled.'

Jessie's cheeks flushed with colour and she gave a
diffident shrug. 'No, it's nothing. It's just…' She broke
off.

Katie frowned. What was going on in Jessie's head?
She was usually so forthcoming but now she was being
uncharacteristically reticent.

'Are you bothered about me being with Ross?'

Jessie hesitated. 'I…I just think it could be a problem for you.'

'How? What do you mean?'

'Well…' Jessie was flustered, and it seemed to Katie
that she was searching for a way out of the situation.

Something was clearly on her mind, but apparently she wasn't quite ready to share it with her.

Instead, she said quickly, 'How are you going to explain things to Mum and Dad? You know how they feel about him. As far as they're concerned, he's still the youth who caused the fire all those years ago. He was always in trouble over something or other back then, and I don't think they'll ever trust him. And right now they're upset for you because he came out of the blue and took the job you were going after. They're thinking he could have backed out once he knew you were in the running for it.'

'That was never going to happen.' Katie's mouth flattened. She had the strongest feeling Jessie was sidetracking, trying to avoid saying what was really on her mind. She wasn't even looking her straight in the eye. 'You could be right about everything,' she said sadly, 'but I'm not sure what I can do to help them to see him in a different light. No matter what I say they go back to their original way of thinking.'

'No.' Jessie let out a long, slow breath. 'I don't know what the answer is either. It's an impossible situation.' She started to turn away and headed for the stairs.

Katie was puzzled. Jessie's reaction had taken her by surprise, and she couldn't think what accounted for it. After all, her sister liked Ross. She'd always liked him, and Katie would have expected her to be happy at the news that she was in love. Unless…

The truth dawned on her gradually, and Katie began to feel sick and dizzy all at once. All those times Jessie must have bumped into Ross at McAskie's, the times when she'd been quiet and withdrawn just lately.

Had Jessie fallen for him? It could happen so easily after all, given Ross's easygoing manner and his inherent charm. Jessie was unattached, and Ross was every woman's dream.

It was the worst thing that could have happened. What was she to do? She couldn't bear to see her sister hurting.

CHAPTER TEN

'How DID YOU find the boy, Dr Brechan? Was it a race against time to get him to the hospital? He's still in Intensive Care, isn't he? How's he doing?' The young man stepped forward. 'I'm James Standish from the *Evening Messenger*. Would you care to give me your story?'

Katie blinked as a camera flashed, and she put up a hand to shield her face as the reporter from the local newspaper came towards her, and his photographer raised his camera once more to take another picture. By her side, Finn appeared bemused, and Baz, ready and eager for his daily walk, looked curiously at everyone, interested to see what was causing the delay.

'I'm not sure what to tell you,' Katie said. 'Yes, Jack's still in Intensive Care and we're very worried about him.' Jack was fighting the dangerous infection that was raging through his body, and when she'd checked up on him that morning, she had been told he was under sedation. 'Actually,' she told the reporter, 'it was Baz who found him.' She waved a hand towards the puppy, who by now was busily examining the cameraman's feet.

The reporter smiled, sensing a new lead. 'He's a bit young to be trailing someone, isn't he?'

'Well, he's a good learner. Finn trained him. He's Finn's dog.'

James was clearly interested in getting to know all he could about the rescue, and the parts Baz, Finn and Ross had played in it. He listened carefully and asked a lot of questions. 'It's been great talking to both of you,' he said after a while. He glanced at his watch. 'If I get this back to the office now, the story should be featured in the paper later this afternoon.'

Katie and Finn watched as the two men hurried away. 'It looks as though fame has caught up with you at last, Finn,' Katie said with a smile. 'I expect there'll be a picture of you and Baz on the front page.'

He laughed. 'Maybe. We'll see.' He leaned down to stroke the puppy. 'Come on, Baz. Heel, boy.' Katie walked with them on her way to the local shop, and he added on a thoughtful note, 'I'll probably not get to see the paper till later, anyway. I'll be going to the barbecue and fair at McAskie's Bar. I think most folk from the village will be there, don't you?'

'More than likely.'

Everyone had been talking about the event, and her boss, Dave Haskins, was expecting her to be there. 'It'll be a great way of getting everyone interested in the new minor injuries unit,' he'd said, 'and you need to be seen to be supporting Ross McGregor. The staff are concerned that you didn't get the job, and they will be looking to you for your blessing on his endeavours. People will be expecting to see you there.'

'I suppose you're right,' she'd said, with a sinking feeling in her stomach. Ross and Jessie would be at the event and she'd no idea how she would handle things. 'I'll be there.'

It was the middle of the afternoon when she set out for the pub, thankful that at least the weather was holding up for the event. The sky was clear and the sun spread a warm golden glow over everything.

The pub was a long, low, whitewashed building, made cheerful with hanging baskets filled with colourful blooms, and all the doors and windows were open to let in the fresh air. The building was bordered on one side by the glittering waters of a loch and all around there were fields, set amongst a backdrop of low hills, and, further away, rugged mountains whose tops were clothed in pale cloud.

People were already making the most of the early autumn afternoon, sitting at tables outside the country pub, where giant parasols shielded them from the hottest of the rays. A gas barbecue had been set up on the terrace and the appetising smell of chicken mingled with that of burgers and pork sausages. In the field beyond the car park stalls had been set up, offering produce for sale, fruit from gardens, home-made preserve, and handcrafted goods of all kinds.

Katie mingled with the crowd for a while, talking to friends and stallholders and making the occasional purchase. She spotted Josh among the crowd, and he came to join her later when she was standing by the waterside.

'Have you seen anything of Ross?' he asked. 'I particularly wanted to talk to him.'

She shook her head. All the time she'd been walking around she'd been looking to catch a glimpse of him. 'Someone said he went to sort out a problem with the gas canisters for the barbecue. Apparently, Jessie went with him.'

'Hmm.' His mouth twisted. 'I heard they'd been together for most of the morning.' He didn't seem to be too happy about that.

Katie didn't comment, not wanting to pass her own

misgivings on to Josh, but instead she looked out over the loch while he went to buy drinks from the bar.

He came back a few minutes later with ice-cold lagers in tall glasses, and walking not far behind him were Jessie and Ross. Katie's mouth went dry. How was she going to face either of them?

'Hi, Katie.' Ross came to join her, watching the wildfowl dart in and out of the reed beds, searching for food. 'I'm glad you managed to get here.'

'Hi.' Katie tried her best to appear composed, when in fact she was nothing of the sort. 'Did you manage to fix your problem with the gas canisters?' He and Jessie seemed to be at ease with one another, though Jessie's expression was a little strained, and she couldn't help wondering what had gone on between them.

He nodded. 'Yes, they'd both run out and there was a hitch when the chef tried to find new ones to replace them. Everything's fine now, though. Jessie helped me to change them, so the panic's over and the barbecue can go on.'

'That's good.' Katie's brows drew together. 'Though everything looked perfectly under control to me—I'd no idea things had gone wrong behind the scenes.'

'Well, hopefully that's the worst of it. There have been so many last-minute hitches—Jessie's been helping out all morning and we've hardly had a moment to ourselves, let alone a chance to stop and chat. I think we've earned the chance for things to go smoothly for a while.'

Ross bent down and picked up some sycamore wings that had fallen from a nearby tree, and began to deftly skim them through the air and out over the water. He appeared to be completely relaxed, though Katie was more confused than ever.

Jessie held out her hand to him and he passed a few

seeds to her so that she, too, could send them into flight and watch them spin.

'You must have been worried sick,' Jessie said, glancing at Katie, 'when you found you were stranded last night. I can't imagine how I'd have managed if that happened to me.'

'You'd have done the same as Katie and made your way to the bothy,' Josh responded. 'And, of course, I'd have gone along to keep you company.' There was a glint in his eye. 'I expect that place could tell a few tales if it could speak.'

Jessie's brows lifted. 'I don't know what you're imagining, Josh Kilburn, but you can censor it right now.'

Josh's grin was wider than ever. 'That's easier said than done,' he murmured, and she gave him a quizzical glance, before turning her attention to Ross.

'I think it must have been awful for Jack, being away from home and in so much pain,' she said. 'It was lucky for him that you were there and had all your medical equipment to hand. You and Katie saved his life.'

'I certainly hope so.' Ross pulled a face. 'I won't be able to relax until I know he's out of Intensive Care.'

'I asked his parents to let me know how he's doing,' Katie said quietly. 'Freya's not been home since he was admitted to hospital, and Harry only came back for a few minutes this morning to collect some pyjamas and toiletries for him. I heard the grandparents are looking after their little girl while they're spending time with Jack.'

Ross nodded, and glanced across the field to where Finn was walking Baz. There was a girl about his own age by his side, and Ross waved to both of them.

'He looks happier than he has done in a while,' Katie

commented, waving along with him. 'Perhaps he has a girlfriend to cheer him up.'

'There is that—he met up with her on your father's estate, apparently,' Ross answered with a wry smile, 'or it could be the article in the local paper that's given him a boost. The landlord has a copy in the bar and it looks as though Finn and Baz are front-page news.'

'Well, that should make your father feel a bit better towards him, surely?' Katie finished off her lager and set her glass down on a table close by. 'Perhaps you should show him a copy of the paper?'

'There's no need. They have it delivered.' Ross grinned. 'I've been telling my father he needs to give Finn the benefit of the doubt sometimes, that he's a good lad. Maybe now he'll believe me.'

'You've been talking to him? That's something new, isn't it?' Katie was surprised and pleased at the same time.

He nodded. 'I took your advice and went to see him again. I knew what you said made sense.' He shrugged. 'It was difficult at first, as I knew it would be, but Stephanie was on my side and acted as go-between. Now that she's feeling better in herself, she seems to be much more focussed, and she kept trying to tell him that he'll drive Finn away if he doesn't ease up a bit. Of course, he's still worried about this business with the break-in. It's been weighing on all our minds.'

'I wanted to talk to you about that,' Josh put in. 'I had official confirmation this morning—they're not going ahead with the prosecution. Not of Finn, anyway. They said there wasn't any evidence against him. No fingerprints, nothing to show that he had been inside the perimeter of the building, or the building itself, whereas the other boys left fingerprints, shoeprints and other signs that they'd been there. Finn made the mistake of being in the wrong place at the wrong time.'

'In more ways than one, when you consider the damage the dog did to his ear.' Katie gave a sigh of relief, and Ross raised the palm of his hand and gave her a high five, exulting in the good news.

'That's a great result, Josh,' he said. 'Does Finn know?'

Josh nodded. 'I phoned him about an hour ago, as soon as I heard. It was lucky I went into the office this morning to go through the mail or he wouldn't have known till Monday.'

'That's brilliant.' Ross's gaze strayed to his brother once more. 'No wonder he looks so happy. All his troubles are over.'

'Except for the problem of the puppy,' Jessie said with a frown. 'He loves that dog to bits, but Baz is never really going to belong to him unless he can persuade your father to let him stay at the house with him.'

'That's true.' Ross made a face. 'I haven't worked out how to get round that one just yet.'

On an impulse Katie ran a hand lightly down his arm. 'I'm sure you'll think of something.' She felt a sudden need to touch him and show him that she would support him in any way she could.

He laughed. 'You seem to have a lot of faith in me.'

'I do.' She gazed up into his eyes, loving his warm, responsive smile, but then she felt Jessie's stare boring into her and she quickly looked away.

'Why don't you and I go and look at the home improvements stand?' Josh interjected, placing a hand under Jessie's elbow. 'You said you were thinking of getting some new furniture for the extension you're having built—from what I've seen, they've some great ideas here for furnishing conservatories. You might be able to pick up some ideas.'

Jessie frowned. 'Oh, I thought I might stay here with Ross and Katie, and maybe get some lunch. We haven't really had a chance to talk…'

'We can get something to eat in a while. I'll treat you to a medium-rare steak—that's what you like, isn't it?'

'Well, yes, but—'

'I can't stay around anyway,' Ross intervened. 'I have to go and organise the raffle and make sure everything's in order for the horse-riding sessions to start in around half an hour.' He glanced at Katie. 'I hoped you might like to come and help with that. The horses are on loan to us from your parents' stables after all.'

Katie nodded, but Jessie said with a frown, 'Don't you want me to come along and help? They're my parents too, you know.'

Ross gave her a thoughtful look. 'I realise that, Jessie, but Katie and I work together and we need to present a unified front here for all the sponsors. Perhaps you and Josh could join us later to try the horse-riding? We've marked out a route through the country lanes and across fields. It should be fun.'

'Okay.' Jessie seemed doubtful. She clearly wanted the chance to be with Ross and maybe talk to him about what was on her mind.

'We can be back in half an hour,' Josh promised, giving Jessie an encouraging smile. 'Ross can put our names down for first dibs with the horses. Like he says, it should be fun.'

Jessie nodded, and they walked away towards the field where the stalls were set out. Katie glanced at Ross as they, too, left the waterside and headed over to the table where the raffle prizes were set out.

'I'm worried about Jessie,' she said softly. 'She's not been herself lately. It's as though there's something on her mind. I get the feeling she wants to talk to you.'

'Do you think so? It's true we didn't get the chance to talk much this morning. There were a lot of people around.' He frowned. "Do you have any idea what the problem might be?'

'Not really.' She wasn't going to tell him about her fears. Whatever Jessie had to say to him was between the two of them, and perhaps she would find out later when they had sorted it out. Whatever the outcome, she only hoped it wouldn't cause a rift between Jessie and herself.

A crowd gathered around a few minutes later as Ross alerted everyone to the drawing of the raffle, and when he had given out the main prizes—a digital radio, a food hamper and a bottle of wine—he announced that the horse-riding sessions were open to those who wanted to book them. 'The animals are all used to being ridden,' he said. 'They're quite docile.'

There were more than a dozen horses in all, including several ponies suitable for children to ride. 'We have instructors on hand to help people who are inexperienced,' he said, 'and those riding sessions will take place on the field. But if you're used to riding, you can take the country-lane route. There will be experienced riders on hand to supervise.'

Josh and Jessie came to join them by the gate where the horses were assembled, and a girl came forward to tell them about the route they would take. 'Someone will ride along with you to make sure all is well,' she said, but Katie told her that wouldn't be necessary.

'My sister and I are used to these horses. I'm sure we'll be fine.'

Jessie seemed a bit more relaxed now, and Josh was smiling, so she guessed things had gone reasonably well for them and he had somehow managed to coax her out of her sombre mood.

Josh went to pick out his horse, and it looked as though Ross had made up his mind to take advantage of his temporary absence. He went over to Jessie and took her to one side, his expression serious, and Katie felt the breath become stifled in her lungs. They moved away from her and talked quietly for a few minutes, and even though she couldn't hear what they were saying, Katie felt awkward, worried about her sister's well-being.

Frowning, she busied herself by going over to her horse and stroking him, and generally trying to put him at ease. She talked to Josh about his mount, a beautiful stallion, an Arabian chestnut. All the while it bothered her that Ross and Jessie were still talking, and Jessie's expression was increasingly tense.

'There are signs along the lane warning road users to take care while there are riders about,' the instructor said after a while, 'but usually there is very little traffic in this area. People coming to or from the pub mostly take a different road. Take care, anyway, and make sure you ride in single file.'

After a few minutes they set off, kitted out with hard hats loaned to them by the stables, and they let their horses find a gentle pace that suited their country-park surroundings. Josh and Jessie were in front, and Ross brought up the rear.

They passed wild blackberry brambles that were ripe with fruit, and Katie commented it was a pity she and Jessie hadn't thought to bring baskets with them. 'We could have made half a dozen apple and blackberry pies and stocked them in the freezer.'

'Sounds like heaven to me,' Ross murmured. 'Blackberry pie with ice cream, blackberry pie with custard, blackberry pie with fresh cream...'

'I think we get the idea,' Jessie said. 'You can come over to my house and have supper one day. I'll make a pie especially for you.'

'Don't I get an invite as well?' Josh asked in a plaintive tone. 'I'm partial to apple and blackberry pie, too, you know.'

'Hmm. I'll think about it,' Jessie commented.

'Is it that difficult for you to decide?' Josh grumbled, teasingly. 'You owe me, anyway. Who was it who put your builders straight the other day?'

'Oh, well...in that case...'

They ambled along the lane, chatting about this and that, taking in the fresh, country air and absorbing the beauty of the hills and valleys all around. Jessie was subdued, but it was obvious she was trying to join in with the generally laid-back spirit of the occasion.

Katie began to cheer up as Ross talked to her about the familiar landscape, pointing out features that he'd missed through all his years away from the island.

'Do you remember that weir?' he asked, and she nodded, smiling at the memory.

'We used to stand on the bridge and race small sticks in the water. They were happy times.'

'They were.'

They stopped for a while in a lay-by next to a large wooden gate so that they could drink in the view across a meadow covered with wild flowers and take in the smooth expanse of a distant loch. The girls stayed close by the gate while Ross drew his horse into the shade of the hedgerow, where a silver birch vied for space with hawthorn and alder.

Ross leaned closer to Katie. 'Look,' he whispered, his head next to hers so that his cheek briefly brushed hers, 'there's a grouse hiding in the heather. Do you see his reddish head?'

Katie followed the direction of his gaze, trying to ignore the warm, contented feeling that surged inside her at his touch. 'Oh, yes, I see him,' she said in a low voice. 'He's so plump, isn't he?' She was fascinated, watching the bird, who stayed perfectly still in the undergrowth. He had a bill that was slightly hooked at the end, and he sat there, unblinking, watching them watching him. Then suddenly he rose up into the sky with a great flapping of his wings and eventually disappeared from view.

Katie turned to see if Jessie and Josh had seen him, too, but as she twisted around in her saddle she heard the noise of an engine and caught sight of a car coming round a bend and along the lane towards them.

Music was blaring from its radio, getting louder as it grew nearer, and Josh's horse was clearly spooked by it. He began to move restlessly. When the car passed them, the sound was deafening, and Katie's expression turned to one of horror as the horse reared in panic.

Josh tried to calm his mount but it was all in vain. No matter how hard he tried, there was no stopping him. Ross acted quickly, catching hold of the reins in an attempt to restrain the frightened horse, but it was already too late. The animal bucked and twisted, throwing Josh off his back and into the air.

Jessie looked on in shock. 'Oh, no, Josh.' She gasped as he hit the ground, sprawling partly into the hedge and over the dry, grassy ditch. 'No, no…this can't be happening.'

They all dismounted and hurried to see if Josh was all right. Jessie knelt down beside him while Katie checked his breathing and circulation and Ross tried to bring the horses under control. They were all agitated now, whinnying, their nostrils flaring, tails swishing. Ross spoke quietly, stroking Josh's mount, gently soothing him, and then he tethered three of the horses to the gate.

'He's unconscious,' Katie said anxiously, looking to see how badly Josh was injured. 'He must have banged his head on a branch when he fell. I think the hat would have protected him to some extent, though.' She pulled open his shirt so that she could monitor the rhythm of his breathing, and when she'd finished, she looked up at Ross. 'I think it's a flail chest injury,' she said. 'I'm afraid a rib might have punctured his lung.'

'Ring for an ambulance,' he told her. 'I'll go back to the pub and get my medical kit. We haven't come far, and with any luck I should be back here before the paramedics arrive.'

'Okay.' She nodded, anxious about their injured friend, desperately hoping that they could help him to breathe more comfortably and restore him to consciousness.

Ross spurred his horse to a gallop and soon disappeared from view. Jessie said unhappily, 'What does it mean, Katie? What's a flail chest? Why won't he wake up?'

Katie finished making the emergency call. 'It means a segment of his ribs has broken away from the chest wall and is moving independently,' she explained. 'The broken section is stopping his chest from expanding properly. And at the moment it's worse because it looks as though a rib has punctured the lining around the lung. Air or blood may have entered there and that will put even more pressure on it and prevent him from breathing.'

Jessie gave a small sob, her face pale and tearstained. After a moment or two, though, Josh's eyelids began to flicker, and then he said breathlessly, 'What's happening?' He tried to move, and gave a sharp moan as pain coursed through him.

'Try to stay still, Josh,' Katie said, thankful that he had regained consciousness but afraid that he might hurt himself even more. 'We're going to take care of you.'

Jessie held his hand between hers. 'You'll be all right,' she told him. 'You had a fall, but the ambulance is on its way, and we're going to get you to hospital.'

He tried to move his head to see where he was. 'Am I…in a…ditch?' he asked haltingly, gasping for breath.

'Yes, sort of, but don't worry about that. We'll get you out.' Jessie lifted his hand to her cheek, holding onto him as though she was afraid to let him go. 'I'm so sorry this has happened to you,' she said. 'I'm so sorry I was mean to you. You know I was only teasing, don't you?'

Josh gave a wan smile. 'Is this…what it takes…to get you to notice me?' He closed his eyes, struggling for breath, and Katie moved in to check his pulse. It was fast and erratic, and she was very much afraid he was going into shock. If only Ross would come back with the equipment they needed—she felt so helpless like this.

A moment later she heard the sound of a car heading towards them from the direction of the pub, and relief washed over her when she saw that it was Ross who was driving. He had with him three of the girls who had been supervising the riding sessions.

'They're going to ride the horses back to the field,' he told Katie.

'That's good.' They handed over their riding hats and the girls quickly led the horses away.

Ross went over to Josh. 'Hey, there,' he murmured,

kneeling down beside him. 'I'm glad you're back with us. I knew your skull was too thick to be badly damaged.'

Josh gave a weak smile, but he was obviously in great pain and closed his eyes once more.

Ross opened up his medical kit. 'Do you think you could hold the oxygen mask in place, Jessie?' he said, and she nodded, eager to help in any way she could.

'Josh, I know you're in a lot of pain,' Ross said. 'We'll give you something to help with that. I'm also going to put a tube in your chest to relieve the pressure on your lung. I'll use a local anaesthetic, so that will make the procedure more comfortable for you. Are you okay with that?'

'Fine,' Josh muttered, clearly in too much discomfort to really care how it was done. 'Do what you have to.'

Katie began to swab the area with antiseptic in preparation, and when she had finished, Ross started the process of inserting a chest tube. They glanced at one another. She could see he was worried about Josh, and filled with regret that a day that had started out with such promise had turned out so badly in the end. For herself, she was anguished that their friend was in such a bad way.

While Ross worked, Katie prepared the drainage bottle that would act as a seal, allowing air and blood to drain away into water but preventing its re-entry into the chest.

'That seems to be in place properly,' Ross said, after a while. 'It looks as though it's draining freely.' He looked at Josh. 'How are you doing?'

'That feels much better, thanks.'

'Good. Once you get to hospital, they'll probably do a CT scan to find out what's going on in your chest and to check that the chest tube is in the right place. They'll keep you in for a few days and give you painkillers.'

Katie helped him to clear away the equipment while Jessie talked to Josh and tried to bolster his spirits. He was still in the same position where he had fallen, but when the paramedics arrived a couple of minutes later, they all helped to get him on to a stretcher.

'I'll go with him in the ambulance,' Jessie said, as she and Katie stood to one side while the men transferred Josh to the vehicle. 'I feel terrible about what's happened. I never realised I could react this way. Josh has always been there, our friend, through all these years, and it's awful to see him hurt.'

'I know,' Katie said, putting an arm around her sister. 'We all feel the same way. We've been friends for such a long time.'

Jessie wiped away her tears and looked at Katie. 'I was amazed, watching you and Ross work on him. You were a team—you worked together so well, knowing what to do, what the other needed, without having to say anything.'

Katie smiled. 'It's what we're trained for,' she said softly, but Jessie shook her head.

'It's more than that, I think. I can't quite put my finger on it, but everything went so smoothly, as though you were interpreting each other's thoughts.'

'Well, that happens, too,' Katie murmured. But Jessie was right, she reflected. She'd known what Ross had been thinking as he'd treated Josh, and it was more than possible he'd had the same experience with her.

Ross went over to the ambulance as Jessie prepared to leave a minute or so later. 'Try not to worry,' he told her. 'They'll take good care of him at the hospital.'

Jessie nodded, but her brave attempt to remain calm

crumbled, and she leaned towards Ross, tears falling anew down her cheeks. She rested her head on his chest and he wrapped his arms around her, holding her close.

'He'll be all right, Jessie,' he said. Then, as the ambulance driver started the engine, the sound of their voices was drowned out. Whatever Ross said to Jessie seemed to do the trick because she nodded and dashed away her tears and then appeared to pull herself together. She even gave a little smile.

The paramedic indicated that he was ready to go, and Jessie reluctantly eased herself away from Ross. 'Thanks for taking care of him.' Her voice was firm now, and clear. She glanced at Katie. 'You, too, Katie.'

They watched the ambulance pull away, and then Katie and Ross walked to his car.

'This wasn't at all how I expected the day to end,' Ross said quietly as he set the car in motion and followed the ambulance to the hospital.

'No, it wasn't for any of us. Jessie's very upset.'

'She's had a nasty shock,' Ross said, 'and you have to bear in mind that she probably isn't used to seeing people who are injured. We are, and it was still difficult for us.'

'Still, she turned to you for comfort, and you were there for her.' Her voice was flat, she realised, and she pulled herself together, adding, 'I'd like to stay at the hospital for a while, to see how he's doing. Once they've completed the X-rays and scans, and so on, we should generally have a better idea of what damage has been done.'

He nodded. 'Perhaps we could go back to my place afterwards?'

She was surprised. 'The house, you mean? I didn't realise you'd moved in already.'

'I moved in yesterday. It didn't take long. Living at the pub, I didn't have a great deal of furniture or stuff that needed to be transported. Most of the new items are coming along in dribs and drabs.' He turned the car onto the main road. 'It'll give me a chance to talk to you.'

'Oh, I see.' Her voice faltered. She wanted to go with him, more than anything, but how could she go on seeing him when her sister was so troubled? It would be like pouring petrol on flames. She loved Ross, but how could she risk hurting Jessie? She said quietly, 'Ross, I've had a chance to think things through. I...I don't think it would be a good idea for you and me to be together any more, outside work.'

She heard the breath catch in his throat. 'You're not serious?' Ross was stunned. 'You can't be. Katie, what's this all about? What's brought this on?'

'I just feel it would be better that way. It's too complicated for us to be together, there are too many things keeping us apart. You're my boss...we both have trouble putting our faith in someone else...' And in the end he wasn't going to commit to a relationship with her, was he? Was it worth hurting Jessie for a dream that would never come true?

'We can overcome all of those things,' he said in a taut voice. 'It just takes a bit of effort, the will to make things work out.'

She shook her head. 'I'm sorry,' she said, and her stomach was leaden. 'I've made up my mind, Ross. It's over. We can't be together.'

CHAPTER ELEVEN

'How is Josh? Is there any news?' Katie caught up with her sister in the hospital waiting room and handed her a cup of coffee. 'It's from the machine, but it might help to perk you up a bit.'

'Thanks.' Jessie put her hands around the polystyrene cup and took a sip of the hot liquid. 'They're giving him oxygen and he's had a strong dose of painkillers so at least he's not in any pain.'

'That's good. I'm sure he'll come through this all right, Jessie. I know how worried you are about him, but he'll make a successful recovery, I'm sure.'

Jessie nodded. 'That's what the consultant told me. It's just a matter of time and healing.' She put her cup down on a table and looked around. 'I thought Ross might be with you. Is he here, at the hospital?'

Katie's eyelids stung with unshed tears, and she bent her head so that Jessie wouldn't see how troubled she was. Her heart ached for Ross. He'd been devastated by her rejection of him.

'I think so. He was talking to the doctor in charge.' She wasn't going to tell Jessie what had happened between them. It was far too upsetting to recall. It was as though she'd punched him in the stomach and knocked all the wind out of him. 'He wants to follow up on Josh's treatment and make sure everything's being done to make him comfortable.'

'I thought he might do that.' Jessie gazed at her unhappily. 'It was such a shock, Katie. I didn't realise how much I cared about Josh until this happened. I mean… I've always been fond of him, but this…this has shown me just how much he means to me. I hate to think of him being hurt.'

'I know,' Katie said softly. 'I understand. At least, I think I do.' She frowned, taking on board what her sister had said about her feelings for Josh. 'I've always known Josh was a little in love with you, and I thought perhaps you and he might get together some day, but then you reacted so strangely yesterday when you found out there was something between Ross and me and I wasn't sure what was going on. I thought maybe you had fallen for Ross.'

'Oh, no, Katie. It was nothing like that.' Jessie pulled a face. 'I'm so sorry if I gave you that idea.' She sighed. 'I know we need to talk about this—I've been feeling guilty for so long, and I realise now it's time everything came out into the open at last.'

'Guilty? What can you possibly feel guilty about?' Katie was bewildered by this turn of events, but Jessie's expression was so serious that she knew it was something she needed to hear. She braced herself for what was to come.

'The thing is, it's about what happened years ago… at the Old Brewery. Nobody knew the truth about what really went on. I was so ashamed I kept it all to myself—only Ross and I knew what went on that night.'

Katie stared at her. 'What do you mean, Jessie? I don't understand. Are you talking about the night of the fire?'

Jessie nodded, pulling in a deep breath. 'The truth is, Katie, I met someone. A man named Craig. He was a few years older than me—I was fifteen at the time, very young and foolish, I realise that now. I fell for him completely. I knew it was wrong, but I couldn't help myself.' She hesitated, nervously wringing her hands.

Katie reached behind her for the upholstered bench seat and sat down. 'Go on. Tell me what happened.'

Jessie shuddered and came to sit down beside her. 'We'd been emailing one another for some time. Then, finally, he persuaded me to meet up with him at the Old Brewery.' She swallowed. 'I thought he loved me, that shows how gullible I was, doesn't it?' She looked at Katie, her eyes wide and full of helpless regret.

'I soon found out that he was only there for one thing, and when I wouldn't give him what he wanted, he turned nasty. He wouldn't let me go home.' She closed her eyes and Katie guessed she was reliving the horror of that night.

'I'm so sorry you had to go through that,' she said, putting an arm around her. 'I wish you'd told me what was going on. Perhaps I could have helped, advised you in some way.'

Jessie nodded. 'I know. I realise I should have said something back then but I was so besotted. I knew what I was doing was wrong, going against everything Mum and Dad had said, but I couldn't help myself.' Her voice trembled and she sat for a moment, looking down at her hands.

'I don't know what I would have done if Ross hadn't turned up. He said he'd found out I was there with Craig, and he'd been worried about me so he came to see if I was all right. They fought, and Ross made him go away.

He said if he ever came near me again he'd make sure he would regret it.'

Katie gasped. 'So Ross was protecting you that night?' She was overwhelmed by the knowledge that he'd done everything he could to save her sister. 'But what about the fire? How did that start?'

'I think Craig started it deliberately, knowing that Ross would get the blame. He must have left for the mainland pretty soon afterwards because I never saw him again. Mind you, that was probably because of what Ross said to him.'

Katie hugged her sister. 'I'm so sorry, Jessie. But why didn't you tell anyone? All these years we thought Ross had done it.'

'I know,' Jessie said in a choked voice. 'I feel terrible about that, but I was so ashamed and humiliated. I was sure Mum and Dad would be horrified when they found out I'd done everything they warned me against. They'd have been aghast if they'd known I'd met someone through the internet and that I'd gone to meet up with him—they were both things that were forbidden.

'Ross said it would be easier to put the blame on him. People already thought badly of him, and what was one more misdemeanour?' She looked at Katie, wide-eyed. 'I know it was wrong of me but I was so scared. If Ross hadn't come along when he did…' She started to shake, and Katie drew her close.

'It's all right, Jessie. You were very young. You need to put it behind you now.'

Jessie nodded. 'I've made up my mind I'm going to tell Mum and Dad. They need to know, if you and Ross are going to be together. That's why I was so worried when you came home last night and I saw you kissing each other. I knew I couldn't let them go on thinking he was bad.'

She gave Katie a searching look. 'It'll be all right now, Katie, won't it? I talked to Ross about it, and he said it was for me to decide, but I think it's the right thing to do.'

'Yes, Jessie, it'll be fine.' Katie said it to reassure her sister but she wasn't at all sure things would work out for the best for her and Ross. Was it too late to put things right between them? She'd wounded him deeply. How would he ever forgive her for hurting him that way?

The door to the waiting room opened and a nurse came to tell them that they could go and see Josh. 'He's comfortable now, but bear in mind he needs plenty of rest, and he'll need to take it easy for a while. .'

'Okay. Thank you.'

They followed the nurse to the side ward where Josh was being treated. Immediately, Jessie went to sit beside him while Katie looked on, pleased to see that he had more colour in his cheeks now and appeared peaceful.

A few minutes later she left Jessie at the bedside. 'I'll come and pick you up later,' she told her. 'I guess you'll be staying here for a while?'

Jessie nodded. 'Don't worry about me. Are you going home?'

'I'm going to see if I can find Ross. I need to talk to him.'

She didn't know what she was going to say to him but somehow or other she needed to put things right. He'd been here in the hospital just a short while ago, so perhaps he was still around.

'He went home,' the nurse told her. 'He looked in on Josh and then went off, saying he'd be back later.'

'Okay. Thanks.'

Katie hitched a lift with one of the doctors who was going off duty. 'I'm going by Loch Sheirach, so I could drop you off there, if you like,' he said.

She accepted, wondering if she was doing the right thing, turning up on Ross's doorstep. What if he didn't want to talk to her?

A short time later she stood in front of his house, gazing around and wondering if she was making a big mistake. She knocked on his front door and waited for what seemed like an eternity for him to answer.

This was her dream home, she reflected, with two magnificent white-painted gables at the front and a long, low extended part to the side. She knew, from her explorations with Ross years ago, that the rooms at the back of the house looked out over the loch. Right now it was bathed in evening sunlight as though it was welcoming her and inviting her to go inside.

'Katie?' Ross had opened the door and looked at her in surprise. 'I wasn't expecting to see you. Is everything all right with Josh? Has something happened?' He looked worried and she hastened to reassure him.

'Oh, no, he's fine. The doctors think he'll make a good recovery. He's strong and fit in every other way.'

'That's good.' He hesitated then stood back and waved her into the hallway. 'Come in,' he said.

'Thank you.' She followed him through a wide, light hallway to a large room that faced onto the loch. It was perfect, with tall, wide windows and a big open fire set into a carved fireplace. There were two pristine, pale-coloured, upholstered settees and a glass-topped coffee table, and set against one wall was a shelving unit that housed a music centre and a large, flat-panel television. In a corner there was a beautiful fern, its willowy fronds adding a cool splash of green to contrast with the muted colour scheme.

'There isn't a lot of furniture as yet,' he said. 'I'm going to need some help with choosing other pieces and I'll probably need to redecorate some of the rooms so that they're more to my taste, but it's pretty good on the whole, I think.' She sensed he was talking to cover the awkwardness of the situation. She had no idea how she was going to explain herself to him and the tension between them was so heavy it tightened her chest and made her throat ache.

'I'll get us a drink,' Ross said, and she had the feeling he was restless and uncertain, needing to be on the move. 'What would you like?'

'A cup of tea would be great.' She needed something hot and sweet to give her strength to face what was to come. She straightened her shoulders. 'I know it must seem odd, after what we said to one another, but I had to come here,' she said. 'I need to talk to you.'

'Uh, yes. All right.' His expression was sombre. 'I guessed there was something on your mind.' He frowned and started towards the door. 'Come through to the kitchen.'

She followed him. The kitchen was magnificent, well fitted out with oak-fronted units and wall cupboards, and dark granite worktops that had a hint of some sparkling crystalline substance throughout.

'Sit down,' Ross said, inviting her to take a chair by the oak table.

'Okay.' She did as he suggested, glancing out of the window, and even from here she caught a glimpse of the calm waters of the loch, backed by low mountains. 'Just seeing that landscape every morning must set you up for the day,' she murmured.

He nodded, filling the kettle with water and switching it on. Then his phone started to ring and he frowned. 'I'll switch it off,' he said, pulling it from his pocket. Then he glanced at the caller display and said in an odd voice, 'It's Finn.'

'Then you need to answer it.'

He nodded. 'Hi, Finn,' he said a moment later. 'How are things with you?'

'Just great,' she heard Finn answer. 'Everything's working out brilliantly. They've dropped the case against me, did Josh tell you?'

'He did. I'm really pleased for you. It's a relief.'

'Yeah.' There was a smile in Finn's voice as though he could hardly contain his elation. 'And that's not all. Dad saw the article in the local paper. He said Baz must be a cracker of a dog to find Jack the way he did. I don't think he quite believed it, but I took him to see Baz and showed him what he can do, how well behaved he is. He says he can come and live with us at the house. I'm well made up, Ross. I can hardly believe it.'

'That's wonderful news, Finn. It sounds as though things are looking up all round.'

'They are. When I took Dad round to Katie's house, we ran into Jack's dad, and he said that Jack was looking much better. His fever's down and his blood tests are good, apparently, so they're thinking he might be coming out of Intensive Care soon. That's great, isn't it?'

'It is. It's the best.' Ross glanced at Katie, and she gave a faint smile. It was good news.

'I'll see you later,' Finn said. 'Maybe I'll bring Baz over to the house to see you some time tomorrow.'

'That's a great idea,' Ross told him. 'I'll see you then.'

He cut the call and glanced at Katie. 'Some things are going right, anyway. Did you hear all that?'

'Yes. I'm really glad for him.'

He switched off his phone and looked at her once more, his expression guarded. 'Okay, you said you wanted to talk. What's wrong, Katie?

'Um, yes. Uh, it's about Jessie.' Katie floundered for a second or two. 'She said… I mean…' She stood up again, suddenly restless. 'She told me about that night at the Old Brewery. She said you went there to help her.'

'Ah, yes. She told me she wanted to bring it out into the open. That's right. I went there that night because I was worried about her.'

'But how did you know she'd be there?'

'I was at the pub, drinking, and this man's friends were there, hinting at some sort of bet that was going on. They'd dared him to take her there, and I just knew deep down that she would be heading for trouble. She was very young, completely innocent, and I had the awful feeling it would end badly. I couldn't stand by and let her be taken in by him. I had to go and get her out of there.'

Katie let out a long, slow breath. 'So she was right. You went there to rescue her?' She shook her head. 'I can barely take it in. What happened?'

He pulled a face. 'It was exactly as I'd suspected. He went there with an ulterior motive, and when she found out what he really wanted, she was shocked and upset. He wasn't about to let her go so I saw to it that he had no choice.' His jaw tightened.

'He took it badly, as you might expect, and I think that was why he set fire to the outhouse, thinking that I would get the blame for it. He was right, wasn't he? Some other teenagers arrived soon after the blaze started and he had apparently disappeared by then so who else would they look to for the culprit?'

Katie's eyes widened. 'Oh, Ross, all this time people have thought badly of you and you've had to bear that, knowing what you do…' She gave a shuddery sigh. 'Thank heaven you were there for Jessie that night. Who knows what might have happened otherwise? We owe you so much.'

He shrugged. 'It didn't seem such a big thing at the time. Jessie was afraid of what your parents would think. It was one thing for them to accept she was meeting up with me, that wouldn't have come as too great a shock after all.

'We weren't sweethearts, just youngsters getting up to mischief, but it was something altogether different for them to find out she'd been so gullible and to discover that she'd secretly arranged to see a man she barely knew, except for what she'd read about him on the internet. They'd warned her many times about the folly of doing something like that, and she guessed she would be in big trouble.'

He breathed deeply. 'And, of course, she was worried about the effect on your father's health. His angina wasn't under control at that time, and it could have turned out very badly for him.'

She gazed up at him, her green eyes troubled. 'So you've taken the blame all this time…and I…I was taken in, along with all the rest.' She pressed her lips together in anguish. 'I had my doubts about you starting the fire but I was afraid there might be some truth in it and I couldn't come to terms with it in my mind. I wanted to believe in you, and open my heart to you, but I was anxious all the while about what my parents would think. Can you ever forgive me for that?'

'There's nothing to forgive, Katie. I know you said it was over between us, but it doesn't alter the way I feel about you. You can't do anything to make me think badly of you.' He gently stroked her cheek. 'I love you. That's the truth of it. And I think Jessie knows that, which is why she decided to come clean about everything. She didn't want this hanging over us. I think your parents will understand, don't you?'

She nodded. 'You love me?' She gazed up at him. 'You don't know how I've longed to hear you say that. I was so afraid that you could never want me the way I want you.

'I love you, too…but when Jessie found out, she went quiet and she was so troubled I started to worry in case she felt the same way about you. I knew it would tear us apart. She's my sister, and I couldn't let that happen… not if you didn't love me in return.'

'But I do, Katie. And Jessie doesn't feel that way towards me. There's never been anything between us.' He wrapped his arms around her, drawing her close, and she laid her head on his chest, loving the feel of him.

'I love you,' he said softly. 'It's always been you. I was so afraid that you wouldn't want me, that you didn't feel the same way, and in the beginning I tried to fight my feelings for you, pretending to myself that I only wanted some light-hearted fun. I had to protect myself from being hurt, but when you told me it was over, it was as though you'd cut me off at the roots. I knew I couldn't live without you.'

She gave a small, shuddery sigh, hardly daring to believe he was saying what she'd always longed to hear. Her fingers traced a path over his chest. 'I hoped that was how you felt but you never actually said the words.

I was desperate to hear you say you loved me. But you never did.'

His arms tightened around her and his blue gaze meshed with hers. 'No, but I thought you must know how I felt about you. I tried to show you, so many times, when I asked you out, or fixed your roof, even when I came after you when you were stranded. I did those things because I love you.'

He kissed her tenderly, and all the while his hands caressed her, shaping her curves and bringing her ever closer to him. 'But at first you tried to keep me at arm's length, and I was afraid you didn't care for me.'

'But I do, Ross. I love you.' She said it in an anguished voice and then pressed her lips together briefly. 'I love you so much. But I was afraid. I tried so hard not to fall for you because I was sure you would leave me high and dry, and I didn't want to be hurt.'

'I felt the same way, to begin with.' His voice was husky with emotion. 'I never wanted to fall for you and suffer that awful pain if you should ever leave me or tell me you didn't feel the same way. But over time I started to get the feeling that you cared for me, too, that you might actually love me, and I couldn't take the risk of losing out on that.

'It was too precious, and I was trying to find the right time to tell you. You're my soul mate, the one woman I want to share my life with.'

Her fingers trembled as she ran her hands over his chest. Her heart swelled with love for him and his words had brought a lump to her throat. 'I'm so happy,' she murmured. 'I didn't think I could ever feel this way, so content, so full of joy.'

'Me, too.'

She slid her arms around his waist. 'It feels terrific to have all that guilt and anxiety lifted from me,' she murmured. 'It was so hard for me, wanting you all the time and yet trying to keep some barriers between us.'

'You don't know how good it makes me feel to have you in my arms, Katie. I feel as though I've waited an eternity for this moment. I always loved you, deep down, but you were way out of my reach for so long. You were the girl from the grand house and the big country estate, and you might as well have been a thousand miles away when it came to me telling you how I felt about you.'

He frowned. 'Even all those years ago I wanted you so badly but I couldn't stick around. What with the problems at home and you being the prettiest, most unavailable girl on the planet as far as I was concerned, I had to leave.'

'But I'm so glad you came back.' She snuggled against him, burying her face in his shirtfront, breathing in his subtle, pleasing male scent.

'So am I.' He captured her lips once more and they kissed with passion and reverence for what they had found and with all the exhilaration that came from being together at last.

'I love you so much,' she said again, and he held her to him, hugging her fiercely as though he would never let her go.

'Will you marry me, Katie?' he said urgently. 'Please say yes. I don't ever want to lose you. I bought this house because I know you love it so much, and I'm certain we could be so happy here. You'll make my life complete if you'll only say yes.'

'Oh, yes, please,' she murmured, sighing happily as

she nestled against him, and they kissed again, holding one another in a blissful a celebration of finally being together. It would be for ever, she was sure of it.

* * * * *

A sneaky peek at next month...

Medical Romance™

CAPTIVATING MEDICAL DRAMA—WITH HEART

My wish list for next month's titles...

In stores from 7th June 2013:

❑ NYC Angels: Making the Surgeon Smile
   — Lynne Marshall

& NYC Angels: An Explosive Reunion — Alison Roberts

❑ The Secret in His Heart — Caroline Anderson

& The ER's Newest Dad — Janice Lynn

❑ One Night She Would Never Forget — Amy Andrews

& When the Cameras Stop Rolling... — Connie Cox

Available at WHSmith, Tesco, Asda, Eason, Amazon and Apple

Just can't wait?

Visit us Online

You can buy our books online a month before they hit the shops! **www.millsandboon.co.uk**

0513/03

Special Offers

Every month we put together collections and longer reads written by your favourite authors.

Here are some of next month's highlights— and don't miss our fabulous discount online!

On sale 17th May

On sale 7th June

On sale 7th June

Save 20%
on all Special Releases

Find out more at
www.millsandboon.co.uk/specialreleases

Visit us Online

0613/ST/MB418

Join the Mills & Boon Book Club

Subscribe to **Medical** today for 3, 6 or 12 months and you could **save over £40!**

We'll also treat you to these fabulous extras:

-  **FREE L'Occitane gift set worth £10**
-  **FREE home delivery**
-  **Rewards scheme, exclusive offers…and much more!**

Subscribe now and save over £40
www.millsandboon.co.uk/subscribeme

SUBS/OFFER/M1

Mills & Boon® Online

Discover more romance at
www.millsandboon.co.uk

- 🌹 **FREE** online reads
- 🌹 **Books** up to one
  month before shops
- 🌹 **Browse our books**
  before you buy

...and much more!

For exclusive competitions and instant updates:

 Like us on **facebook.com/millsandboon**

 Follow us on **twitter.com/millsandboon**

 Join us on **community.millsandboon.co.uk**

Visit us Online Sign up for our FREE eNewsletter at
www.millsandboon.co.uk

WEB/M&B/RTL5

The World of Mills & Boon®

There's a Mills & Boon® series that's perfect for you. We publish ten series and, with new titles every month, you never have to wait long for your favourite to come along.

Blaze.
Scorching hot, sexy reads
4 new stories every month

By Request
Relive the romance with the best of the best
9 new stories every month

Cherish
Romance to melt the heart every time
12 new stories every month

Desire
Passionate and dramatic love stories
8 new stories every month

Visit us Online

Try something new with our Book Club offer
www.millsandboon.co.uk/freebookoffer

M&B/WORLD2

What will you treat yourself to next?

*Ignite your imagination,
step into the past...*
6 new stories every month

INTRIGUE...

Breathtaking romantic suspense
Up to 8 new stories every month

*Captivating medical drama –
with heart*
6 new stories every month

MODERN™

*International affairs,
seduction & passion guaranteed*
9 new stories every month

nocturne™

*Deliciously wicked
paranormal romance*
Up to 4 new stories every month

RIVA™

*Live life to the full –
give in to temptation*
3 new stories every month available
exclusively via our Book Club

You can also buy Mills & Boon eBooks at
www.millsandboon.co.uk

*Visit us
Online*

M&B/WORLD2